When Dreams Come True

Harold Thompson

Assent Books
www.lrpnv.com

When Dreams Come True printed, bound and published by LeRue Press, LLC, in Reno, Nevada.

Editing by Tamara McClure

Book available for volume discounts. Contact the author.

ISBN: 978-1-938814-30-3

Printed in the Untied States of America.

DEDICATION

I dedicate this book of stories to the person who inspired me to write it, I believe it is the Lord Jesus Christ. I have no other explanation for its content, it sure was not mine. I would also like to dedicate this to all those who encourage me to continue writing. It at one time was my pastime, but now my passion.

To my wife Margaret Ruth who I am indebted to for teaching me how to write, who is deceased now for some fifteen years. She still is deeply in my thoughts and heart, and is thought of each and every day of my life. I love the memories of all she did to support me, no matter what it was.

She was my inspiration to always better myself and scolded me when I would put myself down. But more than that also taught me to always take my troubles to the Lord and leave them there. She was a strong believer, a good example, and my best friend. As I write she is always right there in my memories of her. You will probably see her in my writings. Could she be the Mia you will be reading about here in the stories?

To Dick Merwin who has always been there for me, proofread my last book, and wrote the forward in it.

To my two Sons Alan and Lorin, both who have helped me through the good times and bad times too. Alan is deceased now and has gone to be with his Mother and Sister, I miss them terribly.

To my grandchildren and great grandchildren who I love too.

To those that helped me understand how horse therapy

works—and this is a big part of the stories in this book.

Also to my adopted family whose son went through Horse therapy, who the doctors said at his birth he would never be able to run. After his mom found this therapy, at the age of ten he was voted best player on the baseball team.

ACKNOWLEDGEMENT

I will first recognize, the Lord Jesus Christ as this novel would not have happened without Him waking me up one night with a strange name on my mind. It was so strange that I lay awake trying to think about what this meant. A story began to develop, so I got up and started writing. The words were just flying onto the page and just kept going. It wasn't anything I had watched before going to bed, just, as they say "out of the blue."

Next, to all those who have encouraged me to continue writing as I have written other books, but never a novel. I feel so honored to be the one who was inspired to write this novel.

I thank all those who are in my life that have gone through the experiences that I included in this book. Some who were treated with handicaps of all kinds, and those who came from orphanages. I thank the owners of the ranches where horse therapy is used to help those with the handicaps, and to help me to understand more fully its value to mankind. And to those who also allowed me to observe them as they worked with their clients. They have helped my book to be more than just a fun novel, though it is. It is an eye into this valuable treatment few know anything about, including me.

I want to acknowledge my appreciation to the publishers, Janice, Lenore and Kathy, and the expert editor Tamara, who also wrote the forward for this book. To educators who said that the methods used by the teacher in this book to teach the children was fabulous and also said that in the times we live in, it is very important to implement.

So thanks to all who have been a part of making this book more than just a novel, but a handbook to follow and to all those who have seen the value of its content. I always want to include my wife Margaret who taught me how to write.

-From the Author, Harold

*T*his novel was born out of a time when I was going through some very dark times in life and finally gave it up to the Lord. I have learned important lessons, however, and realized that sometimes you have to hit bottom before help comes. I found myself so consumed by negativity that I would go to bed and wake up with the same thoughts. I lost a son to cancer and a week later people were so unkind, accusing me of things I never did. I felt so alone and that's when I asked the Lord to take my burdens away; that night I fell asleep with such peace in my heart.

I woke up the next morning with the name of Milady on my mind. I said, "I don't know anyone by that name, sounds like the name of a race horse to me." Was I supposed to put money on a horse? I laid there wondering what this is all about and suddenly a story started to emerge. But why was I picked to write it?

This felt like a fictional story, but what if it could be true? Perhaps it was just to stimulate thought. I got up and saw that it was three o'clock in the morning, but my conscience told me I would forget it by morning if I waited. In a short time I was captivated and in the story; I lived this from beginning to end. I am still wondering who Milady was and why this was coming into my mind, though I was once a teacher.

It began with an orphan boy who found the Lord and changed his life. I wanted this story to unfold to me, what am I to learn? I have never written anything like this before. As the first chapter ended, I was well into the direction it was going. This is a fresh and an enlightening tale that when read and taken seriously is life changing.

We have lost our way in society, have lost respect and trust, and know little about relationships. Two people have brought me into their lives, their story, and I am so glad they did. It revolves around horse therapy which I have witnessed as being very valuable.

Please join the characters and I in this profound experience, don't miss out on the thrill it will bring you. As the writer I couldn't wait to see the next sequence of events in each chapter. Join me now as we take this journey together.

Harold Thompson Author and dreamer

INTRODUCTION

My name is Harold and I am about to share with you a story so incredible yet if taken to heart could change lives, regardless if you are a Christian or not. It would be my desire that you would come to know the Lord as your Savior through Frank's testimony. Although fictional, the principles are still intact. It came to light through a dream I had, but ends up thrilling my heart from beginning to end. I write stories about my wife and our life journeys, history, but this one is strictly about someone else.

Although I am writing this account, I am totally out of myself. If I were sixty-five years younger, I would love to be this character, he sounds like fun.

The story takes on a flavor of thinking of others before ourselves.

The main character is an orphan boy who is adopted by an older man who teaches him many life-building principles, and for the first time in his life has someone who shows love to him. He is being taught by this man he calls dad how to survive in life. He taught him trades of all kinds just as he had his own sons who are now grown. I would encourage young people to read this book as it is wholesome, though it will be life changing no matter who reads it.

This is not my story, I have only been given the privilege of writing it and believe me, I am honored to do so. In all my life I never imagined being an author, but this, "In Moments When Dreams Come True"—this is a work that goes beyond imagination. It was inspired, no doubt about it.

I hope you will enjoy it as much as I have. It will be helpful if you are a picture person, you will be able to be right in the story then. Have a great journey, and I hope you love horses too.

Harold Thompson, Author

FOREWORD

I met Harold Thompson over the phone one sunny afternoon as I was chosen to edit his book. The publisher told me he was a sweet man and I would learn his writing style as I went along. Of course I had already skimmed the manuscript and could immediately feel the passion not only in Harold's writing, but also in Harold.

When I began editing the text, I could hear his voice saying the words. I gave him a call soon after to introduce myself and I also wanted to see if his voice matched my thoughts; it did.

Harold was so sweet on the phone and I could feel a bit of Frank, our protagonist, in him. He asked me if I knew how the story came to him and I did as I had already read it over. But, I think he was making sure I was committed—I was.

This incredible, beautiful tale came to Harold in a dream. He told me that most of his writing has been autobiographical but this, he felt was the work of a higher power. He woke up at three o'clock in the morning and did not stop writing until sometime around noon. The words poured out of him and, I believe, tells a compelling story from the heart and includes messages of hope, redemption, and the value of horse therapy.

"When Dreams Come True" truly takes the reader on a journey and shows us a simpler time. It makes us believe in faith; faith in people, faith in love, and faith in God. If you are feeling down and want to take a walk, or horseback ride, down a country road into the one of the greatest love stories you've read in a while, this is your book.

Frank and Mia have a deep love and respect for one another that you long for these days. Frank has a love for his students and wants to teach them in a way you haven't seen…probably in decades. These people have heart and soul, and they make you happy.

Thank you to Harold for allowing me to take this journey with him and I promise, once you take this lovely, whimsical ride with Frank, Mia, Gertrude and the others, you will feel yourself amongst friends and perhaps see a bit of hope in the world.

With love and admiration,
Tamara McClure
Editor, nsaen.com

When Dreams Come True

Chapter One

A Lady That Changed My Life

$\mathcal{M}$y name is Frank, and I saw this young lady one day on the road in the countryside. She was pushing her bicycle because it had a flat tire, so I stopped and asked if I might lend a hand. I love driving in the country being a city boy, just to enjoy the smells of clean air and enjoy the view of wide open spaces. She said, "I need a ride to my ranch if you don't mind taking me there."

I was in my pickup so I told her we could put the bike in the back and take her home. Opening her door, I asked for directions but not before asking her name, she said it is Milady. "What a beautiful name, mine is Frank, and I am glad to make your acquaintance."

As we drove with the air blowing through the window, we enjoyed lovely conversation. She told me that her dad passed away some time ago when she was very young, and he left the ranch to her and her mother with livestock to manage. "This was where I grew up and I can't see myself doing anything else," she said.

She was a young lady in her late twenties and as cute as a bug's ear. Her hair was twisted into buns on both sides of her head and there was a kerchief around her neck. Milady told me that she loved riding her bike early in the morning for exercise, before breakfast.

We were getting better acquainted, and I found out that she didn't have a man in her life. It's hard to meet someone, she said, when you are so busy on a ranch like ours. I couldn't imagine that.

So what do you do on the ranch, do you raise cattle? We do she said, but mostly we have a horse therapy business. I had never heard anything about this, so I asked what it was. It's a treatment that is used to help adults as well as children recover from certain handicaps, such as being unable to speak, because of some trauma in their lives.

We have a veteran who has lost a limb, children born with the inability to walk, and all kinds of problems. This has been my life for as long as I can remember. I have been certified to do this and I love it. I guess it has taken over my life and it is the most fantastic life, I can't imagine doing anything else.

She went on to describe the different ones who overcame their disabilities. Before we knew it we were at the ranch, and it was beautiful with a sign at the entrance that read, Milady's Horse Ranch. "That's your name on the sign?" Yes, she said, my mum wanted it to be my place, that I would always love if something happened to her. We are not just mother and daughter, but best friends.

I have to tell you that as a city boy, this warmed my heart. I have not experienced this in my whole life, such compassion for each other as well as to their clients, as I came to see.

As we arrived, I just wanted to learn more about this glorious lady and what she and her mother do. Well, to my surprise I was invited to have breakfast with them.

When I woke up this morning, I didn't have a clue that I would be in for such a special day, something that was going to impact my life forever. One never knows what is going to happen when you just get up in the morning and want to get some fresh air.

I met the mom and she was just as gorgeous as her daughter As I sat at breakfast, enjoying the hospitality of these ladies and having great conversation, I couldn't see myself having to go back to what I just came from. This is the life for sure, what peace and quiet I was enjoying.

But as they say, "All good things must come to an end." That's the dumbest thing I have ever heard. I didn't want it to end. I broke into the conversation and told them that I had today free, and wanted to know if I might stay a while and see how they work with the handicap people.

Now, I have never been on a horse, so this was going to be interesting for me today. We cleared the table and washed the dishes together, then went out and met the ranch hands. Where was this going I thought? Well, I am ready for whatever comes.

I wanted to hear more success stories of them helping people. It was a new experience for this city boy, who had never thought of helping someone else, to hear of others being able to enjoy their lives after this treatment. I can't wait to watch the ladies at work, but unbeknownst to me, I was going to experience it firsthand by helping to clean the stalls of the horses.

I said, I am not dressed for this, so the girls got me some clothes that belonged to Milady's dad. Now I look like a country boy instead of the city boy I am.

Well, so much for the clean air I was breathing before I got into this new activity. I got to see, and even feel, up close what ranch life is all about. They told me a little later that I had been a great help. Truthfully, I will never be the same again.

After cleaning the stalls, Milady and I went on a horseback ride and I learned how to put a saddle on, or did I? No, the saddle was coming loose.

"Oh boy," I said, "how do you get this guy stopped?" Milady just cracked up, but it wasn't funny. She helped get it cinched up and we were on our way again to see some gorgeous scenery. We were back in fresh air now amongst breathtaking mountains and streams.

When we returned from that incredible ride, some people had arrived for therapy. Now I will get to experience what they do firsthand. Not being certified, I had to stay a little distance away so it wouldn't detract from the attention of the person or the horse.

In this case it was a war veteran who lost his leg and was having trouble with balance. I helped him onto the horse and all of a sudden, I was drawn into this new experience as my heart went out to this man. After all, he fought for our country. I was hooked! What a ministry this is to enable someone to once again enjoy something in their life, and these ladies with their helpers also enjoy the fruits of their labors.

This man's name was Jake and you will be able to hear more about him and see his progress as his story unfolds. I am excited to see how this helps him.

I am watching Milady do this work and see the compassion she has as she leads the horse around. She does this so well, I think I am falling in love with her. I never experienced this kind of care for another human being and I wanted to see more. I have been so complacent in my life but today something happened more than just helping a young lady with a flat tire. I saw my life in a different way, through the eyes of these two ladies.

I asked Milady if I might call her Mia instead and she said she would like that. In just one day my life was changed from being "into myself" to being a caring person. Who would have thought when I woke up this morning and just wanted to get out of town to get some fresh air, that something like this would happen?

I am so taken with all this it's hard to imagine that just hours before, I was a selfish person and now my life is changed. What happened to bring this about and why is it so compelling to me? I have a life back in the city, or do I?

I stayed through lunch and dinner then had to get back to the city, though it will never be the same again. I said my goodbyes and both of them said, "You can come back any time, we would love to have you."

Well, the next few days went by and I couldn't get the experience out of my mind, I wanted more of this life. It was running around in my head; what was I to do with what I just went through? Was I to get another chance at getting to know Mia better? I would definitely like that. Was I falling in love with her? How could that be as I just met her?

My job is a teacher in middle school and it's terrific; I love children and they relate to me as well. I thought maybe we could take a field trip to the ranch and show the kids what I saw in helping others. This would take some special arrangements.

I want the children to see how the horses react to the handicapped people and help them to see what I did, and create in these children a spirit of love and care for others. Children today are handicapped, as city life with both parents working doesn't create an environment to see the necessity of getting out of one's self and realize the importance of helping others.

I thought of Mia all week long, and it was the weekend, so I thought I would surprise her and meet her on her bike ride. I got my bike out, put it in the truck, and headed out to be with Mia. I kind of knew where to find her and sure enough, there she was.

I rode alongside her and scared her as she wasn't expecting me to be there, especially on a bike. We talked a while and she said, "There is nothing scheduled for today, so I am going to take you on my long ride instead."

She took me to a lake surrounded by beautiful trees and spring flowers with a fragrance just as breathtaking. There were ducks on the water and deer drinking at the edge of the lake. She did it again. I am in heaven and my mind is filled with love and gratitude for this experience to see through Mia's eyes the greatness of her life, and I want it.

We sat on the grass and talked about the possibilities of bringing my class out to the ranch, to let the kids see for themselves a whole new world apart from what they know.

It was her suggestion to first have her come to the class dressed up in her cowgirl garb, and give them a taste of a country girl. They will love it, I promise.

We went back to the ranch and saw Mia's mother, Gertrude. I suggested she come along with us to view the sunset, it was an exceptional warm summer night. I thought this would be an excellent idea and so did she. This allowed me to see Mia and her mother interact together with me, and take the pressure off the two of us. Neither of us were ready for romance yet; we were going to give it time to get acquainted first.

Gertrude took us to the place where she and her husband used to go. It was very romantic and, of course, lovely too.

On the way back Gertrude wanted the two of us to be alone and said, "Why don't you two ride up ahead as I want to spend a little time here alone, to reflect on the time I had here with your dad."

Feelings run deep in Mia's mom and she is a great example for the two of us. We went a ways off to tie up the horses and talk of future plans for bringing my class on a field trip to the ranch. Mia saw something in me now that she liked and was excited to go forward with the plan. I saw something else in doing this—we would be working together and building a relationship.

I told Mia that I would talk to the superintendent of schools about arranging a time and coordinate with her and her mom. I have already talked to the children and they are excited for the adventure as some have never been out of the city, just like me.

We rode back and found Gertrude sitting on a log with tears in her eyes. She said, "Thank you, kids, for this afternoon; it's the first time since Robert left that I have been here."

The day is mostly gone now and time to think about dinner, so I made a suggestion that I would take them out if that would be all right with them. Both Mia and her mom agreed to do that with me.

This is special to me as we are building a rapport and I now feel like part of the family, you see I lost all of mine. My mother died at my birth so Dad raised me, and then one day he died too. I was sent to an orphanage where I didn't know the love of a mother or the direction of a dad.

I am learning from both of these ladies what I desperately missed, and I just love the fact that they are willing to put up with my lack of how to treat a lady. They are teaching me this skill.

You can see that all of us have handicaps, perhaps even the ladies as they have not been raised in a city, always been country folks. I will get the chance to help them with that, though I wouldn't call it a handicap.

There are no horses or cows in the city just noisy busses and lots of cars. I'm enjoying my time away from that and appreciating a life of simplicity. I think of it all week long while I'm at work and get all excited again. And to think, all I did was give a young lady a ride home, a damsel in distress.

I made arrangements to pick them up one Saturday and show them my world. We were going from one shop to another, they were having a ball and I was enjoying it too. They were so happy trying on dresses and shoes, and thanked me over and over again. This was the first time I had experienced this with women. Each time they put on another dress they would come out and show me.

Mia's mother said that she hadn't dressed up since her husband died and this was a real treat. Likewise for Mia, too, since she was quite young when her dad died. As you can see, we are helping one another in getting much needed balance in our lives. I am so grateful for this opportunity.

Chapter Two
Children experiencing caring people

*T*he time had come for the children to meet Milady (Mia). I was so excited I felt like a kid myself; nothing in the whole world even comes close to this event we are about to experience. I kept looking out the window for Mia to show up, and all of a sudden—no way she didn't—oh yes she did! She rode her horse into town and she is tying it up to a post that the old timers used for their horses.

I said, "Class come over to the window and see what I am seeing. Mia has just arrived." They all came over and you wouldn't believe the excitement in the room. You would have thought that some very important person just arrived to town, and you would be right. My heart was in my throat; this was the greatest gift you could ever give to me.

I fell in love all over again… I ran down to meet her and escort her to the class. Well, something I hadn't counted on was that the whole staff was watching too. This is going to be so much more than I expected as the principal had arranged to have Mia speak to the whole school, he had arranged it all without my knowledge.

He had microphones and went with me to meet this lady who was all dressed up in a cowgirl outfit. And here comes her mom dressed up the same way, she had come in her truck. I fell in love with both of these ladies. They said that it was such a privilege to be here, to support Frank's class in this opportunity to make a difference in these children's lives, but now the whole student body was present.

I had the extreme privilege of introducing these wonderful ladies to the whole school. I was in heaven. Nothing could ever top this, or could it? With tears in my eyes, I said that I was overwhelmed and grateful to everyone for helping to make this the greatest day in all of our lives.

"Mia, would you do us a favor and go get your friend?" She knew what I meant and walked to get her horse, Wonder. She paraded her around so the children could pet her and that started the program that day. Mia got up on the platform, introduced her mom, and gave a little introduction as to what they would be seeing.

Mia and her mom stood together with me and they used me to demonstrate how they use Wonder horse to ease the pain that people with all kinds of illnesses have, and why it is so successful.

It was a surprise to all of us when a limo suddenly appeared while Mia was describing what I was doing with the horse. All eyes were on this car and I wondered who was going to get out. No way, the governor of the state? He heard about this event and wanted to show his appreciation. Then another limo shows up, it's a Vietnam veteran who the ladies have been working with. He is going to demonstrate how he's progressed since having the treatments. This, too, was arranged by the principal.

I guess you know that the school was in for a day with Wonder horse and the celebrities on board to entertain all of us; I wished that my dad had still been alive to witness this. We were just going to educate my class, but what happened next took the event over the top.

Many of the townspeople had heard the announcement over the TV and radio, and they showed up to be a part of this special occasion. Now the stands are full, almost to the ball field.

Remember the veteran? Well, I introduced him and he said he was going to do some tricks and told us that although he lost a limb, he would go to war and do it all over again for our country.

"Kids," he would say, "follow your dreams and don't let anyone stop you, regardless of the handicaps you may have in life." He got up on Wonder and with one leg he stood on the saddle and did tricks that inspired all of us.

This man, before the treatment, told us that he wanted to die but now has a second chance. He said, "I thank all of you for your love and support today."

The governor then spoke from the heart, and we all had tears in our eyes. I will never in my whole life forget this. It made such an impact on the children that parents wanted to know how they could be of help to support such a wonderful work. It turned this town around from drugs and crime to a community of caring people. It's like a fresh new start to living peaceably with each other, it bridged across all kinds of lines. I was grateful to have been part of this.

What could be any better than this you say? Keep reading as this is just the start.

We teamed up with some ranchers in the area where Mia and her mom lived for a weekend when the families could come out and share the day with us; go riding and see some of the most glorious country imaginable. People from all over came and joined in the fun. We ended up calling a catering company to help and they volunteered to furnish all the food for the day. All this because a young lady had a flat tire, I am elated and humbled at what can happen with just a little kindness.

I feel that the Lord opened up heaven to shower upon us such blessings unimaginable, and just laid on the grass reflecting on the joy and satisfaction that has been given to me. As I was thinking about this and wondering what else would come upon us, here comes Mia with a cool glass of iced tea. We sat looking at each other, still in awe at what had just taken place and wondering where to go from here. I don't want to go anywhere, I am where I am supposed to be living in the moment.

For the first time, Mia came and sat very close to me. "What does this all mean?" I thought. I love this young lady so much but I'm not sure where she is with everything. Could this be the start of something so great that it would take us the rest of our lives to enjoy each other? I was encapsulated in the moment and didn't want it to change or leave. Is this going to be the day that I can ask her hand in marriage? I have never been so happy in my entire life.

I told you that my mother died at my birth, so I have not known the love of a woman. I am not worthy of this feeling I have right now. Mia is so close, but I must allow her to make the first step in what could be a wonderful relationship. I leaned my head closer to her and waited for her to make the first move. Wonder was close by eating grass but when I was thinking about Mia, the horse came over and put her head on my shoulder as if to say, "What are you waiting for?" We kissed and I said to Mia, "I don't want to leave where we are, I love you so much and want to spend the rest of my life with you. Will you marry me?"

"Yes, I love you so much too, I can't think of a life without you in it." I said I don't deserve to be as happy as I am in this moment. I want to build a life with you, one I never had. My dad did the best he could, but there were never those moments like a mother's love would be. We held each other so tight. Both of us lost out in having two parents in our lives growing up. We will be forever together and I just want to savor this moment, I don't want it to ever end.

Wonder came over again and lay down beside me and put her head on my leg as if to say, "Welcome, I am glad to have a man in the house finally." I said to Mia that I don't ever want to do anything that would change the love I have for her right now; rather I want it to grow and grow. And Mia said, "I don't know if I could ever love you any more than I do at this moment."

"We will start now, Mia, to get to know each other as I don't know you beyond what I have seen. But what I have seen I love so much and wouldn't change a thing."

"Honey, I feel the same way. I was just waiting and hoping you felt it too."

This is the moment I have waited for and I think God put us together. I will have to finish out this semester and then we can make more plans, but right now I just want to spend all my free time with you.

Now reader, can you imagine what school life is going to be like?

I can't help but wonder what the relationship between

student and teacher will be now. We have become a unit to be all that we can be, no more games just serious work.

My question is what else will the Lord put into the works, as He was the one who put the idea of a special event in my principal's head. No one else could have done that.

Mia and I are still spending time together every chance we get, and our love is growing to be more mature and tremendously respectful. We will not be having relations until we are married, this is how one shows the deepest respect for a person you are going to spend your life with.

As fate would have it, I was called into the principal's office and what he told me blew me away.

"Frank," he said, "I just got off the phone with the governor who asked if I would speak to you about doing the same event in other schools across the state."

"I will have to run this past Mia and her mom before I commit.

"I understand Frank, and I'll wait on your decision."

I called Mia right away. "Mia, you will not believe what has happened since we had that event at the school the other day. The governor wants us to do it again at other schools in the state. I am excited about this opportunity, what do you think about this Mia, are you willing to do it again?"

"I will speak to Mom first before giving you an answer, is that okay?"

"Yes, of course Mia, I know this is going to be quite a commitment for all of us, but you ought to see the difference in the children here now as a result of what transpired the other day. Even the parents are different toward us now, we have full cooperation from them. For many things we couldn't get across before, we are now able to, isn't this great? I will talk to you later, I have to get back to class now. I left the children in charge, I couldn't have done that before the miracle happened the other day."

As I went back to class I can't tell you what a surprise I had, the class had appointed someone to take charge and go on with the lesson—WOW! When I walked in I sat at one of the desks and let the student continue and finish out the class. I commended them just before class was over, for their wisdom in doing this, and thanked the student they elected. I said, "You guys have given me an idea and I will tell you about it tomorrow when you come to class."

I thought all night about how I was going to present this idea I have to the staff, I wondered what their response would be. You see, I want to continue doing what the students came up with and have them elect another student, this time for the day. My thought is, why not instead of them being observers let them be participants. This would revolutionize the educational arena.

The next morning I went to the principal's office to discuss my idea with him. As I presented it to him, he looks over his glasses and didn't say anything right away. Then he got up from his chair and walked the floor with his right hand on his forehead. Finally, he burst out with, "I think that would be a great idea, how do you come up with these things, Frank?"

"Well, Henry it was the student's idea. Yesterday when I was in here talking to you, the students instead of being disruptive decided to elect someone to take the class. It was their idea, and it worked well. In fact, I let that student continue until the end of class which gave him more confidence as I thought he was doing quite well."

After school I went to Mia's ranch as I wanted to discuss the plan I'd called Mia about. When I got there dinner was ready, so my timing was great. "I won't have to cook for myself tonight," I thought.

We discussed all the details and also some of the potential problems about what the governor wanted. I didn't have to persuade them, they had already made a decision to do it.

When we put the subject to rest, having discussed all of the possibilities of problems, I wanted to share how the students took over and taught the class when I was in the principal's office today. Both Mia and her mom sat there almost spellbound in amazement, they had never heard of such a thing and wanted to know more about it. I told them that when I got back to class, the students had elected someone to teach the class. When I entered the room and saw what they had done, I let the student continue and showed him respect in doing it.

As we talked about some of the issues in traveling for long distances, I said I would buy a new horse trailer and have it customized with padding on the inside walls as well as get a tandem axle so it would be more comfortable for Wonder.

"I feel we need to take care of our mayor."

Mia wanted to know what the mayor had to do with traveling in the trailer.

"Oh no, not the two legged mayor, our Wonder horse."

After a good laugh, we discussed more of the details and the ladies said, Frank, "You are going to have to dress the part now."

Now it was time to let the governor and principal know we were on board. The next morning I was early to talk to Principal Henry about making arrangements for the special event.

I wanted to bring the class into this too, as they are showing signs of being very civil minded and I wanted to cultivate more of that in them. I went to the office and Henry called the governor while I was there. I was put on the phone and congratulated for such a great job.

I said, "Sir, I was just the one with the idea, all of you made it what it was, thank you. I can't tell you how this has turned around our city, and the children too. You'll have to come sometime for a tour of our school and town. No drugs, and behavior problems cut a lot, thank you for the opportunity to do this."

I then went to my class, which had just arrived, and after they got settled I told them what had transpired since the horse therapy event.

"The governor wants us to do it again in other towns. What do you all think, do you have any suggestions?"

The first question one of the students asked was if they were included. I said I would make a list of all their questions and answer when I had more information.

1 Are they, our students included?
2 Can we go dressed up in "cowboy/cowgirl" clothes?
3 Could our parents go like last time?
4 Can we write a report on it afterwards?

"These are all excellent questions and I am proud to be your teacher. You're an exceptional group, thank you. Now let's get to our lessons for the day."

If you had told me this was going to happen a month ago, I would have thought you were having a senior moment or something. As I look back on this, I remember it all started by giving a young lady a ride home when she had a flat tire on her bike.

Life is good and I can't wait to get up in the morning now to see what the day will bring. When I got home from school, I started looking for who might have a horse trailer for our needs. I think a fifth wheel would be good. I wonder also if a western clothing store would sponsor us at these events. So I called one store and described what we had in mind, and to my amazement, the storeowner jumped at the idea. He asked if this was going to be for the whole school? I said it is just for my class right now, but if the whole school does that then maybe the parents can help with the expense of it. The store owner was willing to go forward with it now.

Chapter 3
Going statewide

*T*he principal called a general assembly for all the students to explain what was in the works for the near future. Each would be given a bulletin to take home with a paper to sign for leaving the city. Parents are welcome to come on their own.

As the principal was sharing, he said that as a school we are responsible to teach more than just reading, writing, and arithmetic. As a result, we will broaden the activities to reflect this new education curriculum. We will be the first school in this state to implement this into what educators will be doing in the future. This is not about horse therapy, it's about caring for people that can't help themselves. If the horses can do this, then we should be able to do it too. All questions were answered and the student body dismissed.

I got a little busy and was neglecting my new family, so after work today I am going to the country to spend a little time with Mia and her mom. I got there at dinnertime again, so I said that since they weren't expecting me I would just have a cup of tea with them and to go ahead and eat.

"Don't be silly Frank, besides we always set the table for three in case someone unexpected comes, so sit yourself down," Mom said. "Besides, you are family you know."

When she said that my heart jumped, she didn't know how much I wanted to be a part of the family. We are getting so close to each other and I am really enjoying it.

It was still light so Mia suggested we go on a horseback ride before doing dishes. We went out, saddled up, and headed to our favorite spot. And wouldn't you know it, it was a full moon that night and the stars were out in force. I am having a real hard time not just holding her ever so tight but no, that is not showing respect. That will come in time and I pray for the day when it does.

It's a new day and back to work. Perhaps I should rephrase that to say, back to more opportunities. The parents are getting involved in the community now and looking for ways to help people in need. I hear some say that our children are teaching us and it should be the other way around. One of the parents told me that when they grew up their parents ignored those in need and would say, "Why don't they get a job?"

I still say this started by helping a young lady with a flat tire.

My Prayer:

> *Dear Lord, a strange thing is going on here today as I reflect on what has transpired in our city, but there's still a lot of work to do. What is surprising, Lord, is that the churches are not getting the message or getting involved, those who should be setting the example in our community. I believe they will come on board too, we just have to give them time to wake up. After all, they say they worship you, you who gave your life for us. You said, Lord, that you became poor that we might be rich. This is you, Lord, the creator. I am blown away with thinking of that. All right we won't wait on them, it's been put into my heart to do this, and I am in with both feet. I am not doing this for the ladies, nor for me, I see a movement happening here with people helping people. It's all about you Lord, thank you for putting this into our hearts. Amen*

I woke up with joy in my heart, ready to tackle any challenges this beautiful day may bring.

When I got to class, I shared with my students some special announcements from the principal and then said, "Let's vote for another student to share the class today." Robert was chosen and looked nervous as I gave him the day's lesson. I told the rest of the class to get ready because their turn may come up next. They could refuse, I said, but reiterated that this is great training for them and no one would put them down.

I then introduced them to grading each other's papers.

"This is going to be another phase in your experience," I told them, "in helping each other with a different mind-set."

The subject of my class is social studies so this is a hands-on project, but it has another advantage. It allows me more freedom to do the extra work on the activities we are doing since I don't have to spend hours correcting papers.

Mia and I have been spending a lot more time together and I've been helping out at the ranch. They are almost overwhelmed with new clients since the demonstration at the school the other day.

I am now helping with the therapy as they have accepted more of the veterans from nearby towns, and I will soon be certified as a trainer. I have time now to do this on weekends and some after school. I am seeing so much benefit to this treatment that I knew nothing about before meeting Mia and her mom, and they have turned my life around with a passion for helping others. Now they want to pay me, and I just refuse because this is a learning experience and I should be paying them instead. Since I am single and have a great job, I can just look at this as a training experience to expand my abilities.

This new phase in my life has given me a passion and love for children and adults with handicaps. What a privilege it is to enable human beings do be able to function and contribute in their lives, instead of being waited on hand and foot.

We are truly making a difference in people's lives, instead of them just feeling sorry for themselves, we are giving them a way to also contribute to society. We are doing this and people are getting the message. How are they helping, you ask? We have opened up the minds of people that say of handicap people, "Why don't they get a job?" or "How can they with a handicap?" Now maybe they can.

I wake up in the morning so ready to see what I can contribute aside from my job. I know that through the Lord using me I have already made a difference in these children's lives. I am sure they will go on in life and want to continue making a difference wherever they go.

What we are doing is something that has been lost in our country, we have become complacent to the needs of others. It's not about how much we can get, but how much we can give. We may want houses, cars, children, and to go on exotic vacations, but it should be about what we do with what we have been given.

Invite someone to your house for dinner, for example, or take other kids with you when you go somewhere with yours. What if I hadn't stopped that day to help a young lady, where would I be today? I would still be going to a mundane job day after day just to feed myself.

It seems that life has many twists and turns in it and many lessons to be learned. I am now seeing life through those who are disabled and through those who help with that. I have fallen in love with life and the prospects of what life will be teaching me next and it's not about me, that is the greatest lesson I have learned. I have also fallen in love with Mia and just want to be with her all the time.

I will at some point, discuss a date to get married, but for now just want to be used to further the wonderful work they are doing to help people. It seems that when you get out of yourself, you need people to make that meaningful or you might just go back into yourself again, and I don't want to do that.

I got acquainted with some of the ranchers nearby and one is a horse rancher. He knew about what we have been doing and wanted to contribute, so he offered his beautiful horse trailer to use in transporting Wonder to the different places. It was even lined on the inside just like I wanted to have. I expect one day I will be more a part of this ministry and even happier than I am right now, although I don't know how I could be.

As an educator, I feel we have an opportunity to show children a meaningful and rewarding life that they can be a part of. I want to see the right kind of attitude in their hearts, in other words having a mindset that giving will be on the top of their list instead of getting. The selfishness will be at a minimum and relationships will be the basis of what can I contribute. This will be about sacrificing time and energy, it will build strong families.

Divorces happen generally because of selfishness, so that is the secondary subject in my class and it has caught on very well. To really teach this, I must lead by example and bring the children and their families into it. We are having staff meetings at school to implement this new idea into our curriculum. Some of them have even been doing this at home with their families and see the value.

With the parents permission I took volunteers from my class to a nearby town, where there were older people on a limited income, to help with some of their needs. I went, prior to taking them, and checked out some of the prospects so we knew what was needed. They cut lawns, walked their dogs, did minimal repairs to the house, and you know that Mia was right there to lend a hand.

This is so amazing there are not words to describe it, and Mia is incredible with the children. Sometimes I just stand back and watch this amazing woman do what she does. Of course I am thinking ahead to when we are a real couple, meaning when we are husband and wife. I get goose bumps when I think about that. She is showing signs of this to me too, she wants to be with me every chance she gets.

Sometimes if she has a hose in her hand, she will squirt the kids and show that she is a kid too. I am madly in love with her and what that means to me is to show the highest respect to her. The children are seeing this too, and that's just one more value to be installed in their minds, more growth. They are seeing how people react to their kindness and our example of interacting with the people

When I first started teaching right out of college, I was not doing well with the students; I seemed to be yelling at them all the time. There were those who tried to take over the class and there was no respect. You know the phrase,

"You won't get respect unless you give it." I wondered how I could do this; "I can't just let them go on this way, how am I going to see a change?" I found out that it was not up to me; they had to have a reason to show me respect. It was obvious they didn't get the training at home, but I am to teach social studies not change them, that's not what I am paid for.

Well, that all changed when I met Mia that day in the country. I saw something that gave me an appetite to want more. You see it's not about sex; she is a beautiful person inside and out. I saw how she reacted with her mom, they loved each other and weren't afraid to show it, and that dug deep into my heart. I had no family that I ever knew, my father and mother died when I was very young, so I was raised in an orphanage where there was not much love shown to me. This is the first family I have experienced since being in that orphanage. No one to cuddle me when I was sad, just harsh words, "Go to bed."

As we continued to work in the community with the children doing things to show kindness, the people started to show the children kindness too as they interacted with them—making jokes, telling stories to them. This was working better than I had anticipated it would, or imagined. Love for people was the result of our labors. Sometimes the children would come on their own to visit the older people. It seemed too good to be true but moms and dads were seeing a different attitude in their children, and that helped the mom and dad show more love for each other. I can't tell you with just one example how it has snowballed into helping troubled families, who knows where this will lead.

Here we are on another Sunday and work is set aside to rest and think about the events of the past week. I have been going to church with Mia and her Mom, but wait a minute; all of a sudden my class started showing up with their parents.

I would sing at the top of my lungs I was so happy. This was not because of something I did, no, someone else was touching those family's lives. I don't claim any part of this, just sitting back to watch it happen. I know someone is working in me too, I have not known this kind of respect before, and my family is growing.

The three of us were sometimes invited to go to dinner with some of the families, and this grew to include other families too. It seemed that a lot of people were getting out of themselves and becoming close friends. They all got together and planned summer vacations to go camping together and of course, Mia and her mom and I were invited as well.

The first time we did this, Mia and I took our horses and would allow the children to ride on one of them. Sometimes it would be Mia with one of the children and sometimes it would be me taking one. Oh, I didn't tell you that I too have a horse, and he is also being trained to work with the handicapped.

This is a life I never would have dreamed of, especially since there was so much drama growing up. I am learning through those experiences, though, that it was helpful for balance. It is in those times of disappointment that we gain strength and abilities to carry on in spite of the discomfort it brings. There is always going to be someone who will try to hurt you, it's going to be all right though. You see, hurting people hurts people. That's where having someone in your life who loves you comes in to comfort you.

I didn't have that growing up, just had to cry myself to sleep. I don't know what's in store for my life from here, if it's always going to be like this. I am grateful for what I have now, it can only get better from here.

Now I want to show kindness to my students, no more anger like the past.

We've been pretty busy in town helping the unfortunate people and it was time to focus on the event we were asked to do by the governor; a middle school was chosen about fifty miles away. Mia and I went to the school selected for a staff meeting and to our surprise, the PTA members that couldn't make it had already heard what we did at my school so they were ready to do the event, and were excited. They had been following our different ventures and were excited to see this done in their town too. Now we have to train someone to take our place as Mia still has her current clients and I still want to teach, whether in the city where I live or in the small town where the ranch is. Mia and her mom and I will still do the events, but not the follow-up.

They say that change starts with just one person and I am seeing it happen.

The mayor called from the town that wants us to put on the demonstration to see how it was going. Wonder and Trigger have been training along with me, so Trigger and I are now both certified. We have more participants this time to bring.

We are bringing a six-man group in wheelchairs to play basketball along with our veteran, Jake, who has one leg missing, he will be playing basketball too. We just never know what he has up his sleeves, he's been training the guys how to do this in wheelchairs. He sure has changed a lot since we first met him, you know the man who thought his life was over and just wanted to die. He is able to walk now with his new leg, but still has a lot of pain.

We, of course, are bringing my class with us and the school allowed us to use their bus to transport them. The parents also came to support the event; to meet the other parents and students and share what happened in their city after they experienced what we taught.

Our team arrived and unloaded our two stars (Wonder and Trigger), and a committee met us to help direct all the people we brought, as well as the people from the town we were in. It was going to start in the football field area and move to the basketball court, for our veterans to demonstrate their wheelchair basketball abilities. They were placed at the bottom of the stands and our students, with their parents, sat above them.

Up in front on the platform was the mayor, the principal, and student body president from their school as well as ours. There was also Henry our principal, the governor, and last but not least, our friend Jake. Mia and I were in the background until we were announced to come forward for our demonstration.

The local principal was the host and said a few words

showing appreciation to all who came, and then asked for us to appear. We rode up at a fast trot as the crowd cheered. The principal then gave a special welcome and thanks to me and Mia for all we've done to make this event happen.

He told a little about witnessing the changes he saw in the townspeople where we first did this, the new method in teaching students, and a personal note of coming to know Mia and me on our ranch to witness horse therapy firsthand.

"With no further adieu," he said, "I introduce to you Mia and Frank." After applause, I acknowledged Mia and she spoke and thanked everyone for being there then turned to the others on the platform and acknowledged each of them. She then gave me a hug and turned the mic back to me.

First I said, "Governor, please come and share with us why we are here." I sat down and he came to the mic to expound on why he asked for our event to come to this town, and throughout the state as well. He wanted to see if what took place in Frank's school and town could happen throughout the state. He then gave the mic back to me, and I introduced the mayor.

After the mayor spoke and thanked all parties who made a contribution to make this an event we will never forget, I gave the mic to Henry, our principal. He spoke to the fact that in all his years of being in the educational arena, he's never experienced anything that's come close to what has happened in our school. Students are raising up, not only in their grades, but how they respond to their fellow students and to us the faculty. I would now like to introduce to you one of our students, the student body president.

He happened to be one of my students and I was thrilled to see such growth. He shared that through the horse therapy demonstration at our school that not only he, but also his fellow students, saw the value in helping others who could not help themselves. "It was through Mia, Mia's mom Gertrude, and Frank that we learned through their example the need to do this. Some of us students volunteered to do community service and I just want to thank them, on behalf of my fellow students and I, for showing us how to live."

More applause and now, a standing ovation:

I then introduced the class president of our host school to speak. It was a young lady, and she spoke about the expectation of seeing how this event will impact their community. She further expounded on the fact that, "All of us students are going to be asked soon about what we want to do in our lives to get prepared for our contribution in our city and country, also life in general. I am excited about my future." She then sat down to her own standing ovation.

Next I introduced Jake who had been so patient to wait along with his fellow veterans. He took the mic but first greeted all those on the platform, the parents, and all our students who came. As he was speaking and telling his story, he took the mic down to where the other veterans were and introduced each of them.

Jake asked each to give a brief statement about why they are in wheelchairs. After the last one he said, "Now we are going to show you what happens when you forget about your handicaps."

That was the queue for one of the students to get the apparatus we use to get wheelchair patients on the horse. It's hydraulic so they just get on, we push a button, and up they go. We came down off the platform to get Wonder and Trigger; we lifted the first one and then the second. Jake couldn't use the lift apparatus as he is not certified. We got both up on the horses and away they went around the field. Jake still had the mic and said, "They don't look any different from anyone else do they?" After the last one rode and it was really a good exercise, they were ready for the next treat.

Jake said, "You know we all have handicaps, now my team and I are going to prove that if you set your mind to it, there is nothing you can't do."

With all that said, the guys came over to the middle court and were ready to play basketball. Jake was now acting as the coach, he had been working with these men for a while and they love him.

"Okay, you are suspecting something right? Well, we

are not going to disappoint you as our principal is always up to something."

Another bus pulls into the stand area and out comes the cheerleaders from their school. I didn't expect this and neither did Mia. The crowd roared as they ran out onto the court. The team was still in the middle court and the cheerleaders did all kinds of tricks, had special lyrics, and ended by surrounding the team. Some even landed on laps.

You can't imagine this sight and the crowd loved it. The team loved it too, and gave them a renewed reason to go forward with excitement. "You did it again," I said, "Henry, we can't trust you to just be a principal." "I love surprises," he replied.

"Well, where is the school basketball team then?" He said that when all the attention was on the cheerleaders, they got out of the bus the young ladies were in; we planned this ahead of time, he said. "They are over there by the stands. I can't take the credit, it was Jake's idea, just wait till halftime."

The ball was in play and you can't imagine the activity and how the veterans ran the ball down court and got a basket. Again the crowd stood and roared. Halftime came and the school team was out there, the cheerleaders came out again, and now the school band was there. The basketball team from school played with the guys in wheelchairs as if there were no handicap fellows there. The school team could not get the ball so the handicap guys won. It was an honest game these guys were just good, much like the Harlem Globetrotters.

We are thinking of selling tickets for our next event. This was worth paying for and it would go towards helping other handicapped people. I didn't know it but the cheerleaders and basketball team parents were also in the stands. When the game ended, the governor spoke and said this day would go down in history as it taught us to not look at our handicaps as an excuse to not do something.

"I thank each one of you who participated in this demonstration today, this will not go unnoticed. And Gertrude, Mia, and Frank for making us aware of our lack of concern for others, I will take this through my office."

He kept his promise and started legislation on a new bill to financially help the handicapped.

Chapter 4
I have waited long enough

*S*ince I have my own horse Trigger now, Mia and I are doing a lot more things together since I am certified and taking up the slack of more clients since the show.

Many people saw the help the veterans give and wanted to see if it might help their families too. I have to say that Trigger is loving all the attention he's getting, and the brushing down that the children love to do. He gets a lot of kisses and I am jealous, but this is all in the therapy.

One day there was nobody scheduled for treatment, so I suggested that all three of us saddle up and go for a long ride. I just love doing this. We'll take a lunch Mia said, and her mom Gertrude agreed to go too. We saw a lot of deer and other game as we rode along the mountains that were covered with snow at the top of them.

We sat on the ground and ate lunch and then Mia went off somewhere close, just out of earshot. I took this opportunity to ask Gertrude for Mia's hand in marriage.

Her response was, "What took you so long? I have been praying that you would be the one, I love you like the son I never had." Mia came back and asked what was going on. "Nothing, just having good conversation is all." Remember, Mia already said she would marry me, but I wanted Gertrude to be all right with it too.

We got back from the ride and after bedding down the horses, we went in and had dinner. I could do this for the rest of my life, this made up for all that I have lost in my growing up and it is soon to be even better. I sure don't deserve such a beautiful lady with no bad manners. I saw her in all of the different situations possible, and no outburst, no bad word from her lips. I asked Mia out for a special dinner at a fancy restaurant in town.

"I would love that, do I dress formal?"

I said, "You look good in anything you wear, but if you don't mind I would love you to do that, and I will too." I will come Saturday afternoon and pick you up, or do you want to ride Wonder in? Remember, that's what she'd done before to surprise me. "No, you can come and pick me up. I would appreciate it, please."

All the rest of the week I couldn't get her off my mind, even the class noticed. I could hear them whisper something; these are smart kids so they probably even knew what I was thinking. But, they have learned to be respectful of me and didn't say a word.

One day I held my hand up to Mia's to see if my hand was bigger to get an idea of the size ring I should get.

The day came and I was in my black suit with a semi formal white shirt and bow tie. I picked her up in my sports car and, wow, she was dressed in the most beautiful dress and ensemble. We didn't talk about what each of us was going to wear, but her dress was black just like what I was wearing.

Gertrude took our picture but unbeknownst to us, the local press got a hold of us going on our first formal date and was right there to take pictures. Then we were ushered to a limousine that the local paper hired for us.

"This is too much!" I took Mia aside to ask her if it was all right or did she want to cancel the limo.

She said, "Let them contribute, they want to be a part of what we do."

Do you see what I mean about this wonderful lady? She is all that I could ever ask for. At that moment I fell in love even deeper and can't wait until the day we'll be one. As you can see, she is always thinking of others.

The press didn't follow to allow us to have privacy on our date. When we got to the restaurant there was just a single photographer there to take some personal photographs. It seemed that I was both nervous and excited at the same time.

This is my first formal date ever so I didn't want to spoil the moment, it was too special. I'm not a person that likes attention, but I was excited for Mia as she deserves the very best; so I took myself out of it and just admired her. She's so beautiful and loving.

We had a glass of white wine to celebrate this special time together, just the two of us. Her mother would see the pictures later, but the press suspected that we were going to be engaged tonight so they snuck in with Gertrude and seated her where we couldn't see her or them.

Of course these two ladies always did things together, they were more than mother and daughter, they were best friends. We got up and danced and this is the first time we were this close, Mia had worn some great smelling perfume that was messing with my head. I put my face close to hers and then it happened, she leaned in and it was the first time we kissed this deeply.

It was another first but not the last that night. We finished our dinner and in front of everyone, I got down on my knee with the ring in my hand and just then the press began taking pictures; they were right there quietly out of sight. Right then I asked Mia if she would accept the ring and be my wife.

"Yes, I would be honored to spend the rest of my life with you."

Everyone stood up and clapped, and then out of nowhere came this group and played "I Will Love You Forever." Mia got up and threw herself into my arms and we kissed for what seemed to be an eternity. I didn't want to stop and neither did Mia.

In this moment in time there was no one else around, I will remember it forever. She truly became MY LADY that night. Gertrude watched the whole thing from where she was sitting and came over and grabbed both of us.

She said that this was the happiest day in her life. "Now I have a son I've always wanted. I love both of you so much, congratulations! I have seen that when you give, you also receive."

It is true in our case, and both of us were so elated to see such love and admiration given to us. Neither of us felt that our privacy was invaded as we were a part of these people's lives, and always will be. And so for the rest of the evening we danced with many. My second dance was Mia's mom, soon to be mine.

I said, "Mom, I have waited for this moment all my life, when I would have a mother and a wife. Thank you for having such a wonderful daughter. I love you, Mom, so much."

Most of the people there that night were parents of my students. I wondered who might have told them, yep, MOM did. I now write her name in capital letters as she is going to be my mom now and deserves all my respect. I have a mom, wow! Now I am going to learn something new as I didn't grow up with a family, and finally I am going to have one.

I had never had a date with a girl in my whole life, never kissed one. Some say you should date a lot so you know when the right one comes along. I didn't need to do that because no one would ever hold a candle to my Mia. Just think what would have happened if I hadn't stopped that day to help a lady with a flat tire. I think I will put the bike under glass to remind me of the joy that comes when you help someone.

So much has happened as a result of my meeting Mia and Mom; the whole community has honored us tonight and of course, it's time to pay them back.

There were so many flowers that it would almost take a truck to carry them, but they were put into the limo with us. I am so blessed to have a family and a community of caring people now.

We got in the limo and took Mom with us, I held Mia until she fell asleep in my arms. This was such a new feeling and I didn't want it to stop. I was in heaven on earth and

I will remember this moment forever.

Well, it's back to work as usual, but it really isn't work now with the attitude of my class of maturing young people. Again, to get respect you have to give it first — I do love and respect them.

The class came early and as I walked in they all stood up cheering and said, "Congratulations, we heard that you and Mia are now engaged to be married." I asked how they all felt about that and they responded with a heartfelt "We all love both of you so much," while they formed a circle around me.

That afternoon Mia came into town with both Wonder and Trigger, you see we have become family to the young people now. They even enjoy coming out to the ranch and working with us on Saturdays. We are not just student and teacher, we are close friends.

When the class left Mia held me and said, "Honey, you are going to make a great father, you love these kids and they love you." I can't wait to have children, it's been my dream and I can see them all right now in their overalls working alongside of their mom and dad.

I responded by telling Mia that she will make a wonderful mother. "You will be teaching the girls how to make cookies and how to be kind to people, dear, I just love you so much. Let's go on a ride back to the ranch and I can pick up my car."

We have become a legend to the townspeople, they all stop what they are doing as we ride by. It would have bothered me before, now it's a matter of showing respect, so we always acknowledge them too. I am out of myself and see people in a different light now.

We have put the events of going to other schools on hold until we work on relationship with family. Sometimes I have seen people get so busy that they neglect their families, we will continue when it's more feasible to do. I want to show Mia that above all else she comes first along with our children when they come. I never want to do anything that would cause Mia to fall out of love with me. I want it to grow each and every day.

We got back to the ranch and Mom had started dinner already, so we bedded down the horses and went in to lend a hand. We joked and had a great time reflecting on the other night at the engagement dinner.

Mom said, "I hope you were all right with me being there."

Both Mia and I said at the same time, "Yes, it was the way it should have been, we can't keep our lives to ourselves."

With that Mia gave me a big kiss, and said, "I love you." I am coming to appreciate those words so much as I have not grown up having heard that. It's okay, I understand that I was cared for. It was a business to those whose house I lived in when my father died, and I am grateful for what care I got. So now I will appreciate it so much more and not take anything for granted.

We played a few games and had great conversation and Mom said, "You might as well stay overnight and go to school in the morning."

They had a guesthouse on the ranch and I had stayed there many times before, so I said I would do that as I was a little tired. We discussed plans for the wedding a little and then I said goodnight and went to bed.

Mia and I had already talked it over about not having relations before we were married, so we're careful when we are alone to not get too carried away. After all, we're mature adults and know what a great relationship should look like…and that is to think of the other person more than we think of ourselves.

I got back to school the next day, and of course the class asked how the relationship was going.

I said, "Before we go into our studies this morning, I want to share something with you. I consider you students to be mature enough to take in something wonderful about relationships." You see, you can damage them so they will never be repaired again.

'This is what I mean—that you save yourselves and not have sex until you are married. In this way you are showing the future mister or misses that you respect them above all else."

"How many would like to sign a certificate that says, 'I will remain a virgin until marriage'. Raise your hands. Don't be embarrassed, we are not just kids discussing a subject. You see when you do get married, you will be able to give the certificate to your spouse and there will be no better gift that you could give them. All their hands went up."

"I will get the certificates for you to sign; I have one myself on a wall at my house. You can do this as you have already shown that you think of others more than your-selves, right? Now, you girls can talk to Mia and boys you can discuss whatever with me too. We are more than just student/teacher, we are co-workers in building relation-ships." The class all clapped to show their agreement. On a side note, this is an awesome and special group of young people.

What do you suppose happened after that discussion? The principal got wind of it and asked if I would be willing to discuss this with all the boys in school and if Mia would talk with the girls. I said I would be inclined and would dis-cuss it with Mia, but I believe she would be on board.

Relationships with boys and girls is special, they could be building a relationship that would last a lifetime, even if they don't become husbands and wives. But the relation-ship needs to be guarded carefully so it doesn't get dam-aged; it is so easy in a short time to be regretful of circum-stances that could have been avoided.

So Mia and I discussed the possibilities and we com-mitted to do it.

It was a huge success and we got certificates for all the students and had them framed.

We have come a long way from just having an event to show how horse therapy helps people in so many ways; none of this would have happened if it weren't for meeting Mia that day.

I'm sure you're wondering how the parents of the chil-dren took this. Without exception all approved. Some even said they wished they had had a teacher like this when they were in school.

Chapter 5
Building relationships

*T*here's a breeze in the air this morning, singing birds, and the smell of lilacs so pungent it takes your breath away. Everyone is happy as spring has come, the cows have their calves, the deer their fawns, and all kinds of things going on. Also there is romance in the air, even a full moon at night and I have caught the bug. There's nothing you can take for it and you don't really want to be cured anyway. The ladies are starting to put the wedding plans together and they would ask me from time to time what I would like. I just say Mia and they just laugh.

We thought about riding up on our horses with the Vietnam veteran. He will give Mia away, I'll take her off Wonder and hold her hand, then we'll walk up to where the preacher is with the two horses. We will dress them up for the occasion too. But what about the maid of honor and best man?

I said, "Well, they will be up in front to welcome us to the ceremony." Of course we will have it at the ranch, mainly because of all the people who will want to come. We are not restricting anyone, as both the city and country people will all want to there. This is our reward for showing concern and care to all of them. I come into the plan by making all the props.

Some have already donated things, like all of the flowers; others came to help me with the heavy stuff. I'm a guy and all I want is Mia but I am not showing any restraint, all of this is for her and I want to show her how much I love her. Whatever Mia wants Mia gets.

I am already learning some good advice: to have a

successful marriage, you have to think more of the other person than you do yourself. I have no problem with that, I would go to the ends of the earth for Mia.

Our love is starting to grow for each other more every day, and Mia can't do enough for me either. This is truly a marriage made in heaven, and we both feel the blessings of the Lord upon us. I haven't mentioned Him very much through all the special events we are experiencing, but He has been there through it all. It is my conviction He put us together, there is no other explanation for all the things we are experiencing.

You know to me it's not about religion, it's about relationship. I met the Lord when I was still in the orphanage, and one of the good things they did there was to give us all Bibles. I read how God loved me; I found someone who loved me and I wanted Him. I asked Jesus Christ to come into my heart one night as I lay in bed thinking about the one who died for me and wants to be in my life.

One of the first things I did before starting our relationship was to find out where Mia was with the Lord, and she told me her story.

It was when her father died and the preacher at the service said, "If you want to see Jack again you are going to have to accept Jesus Christ and ask Him into your heart."

She said, "I saw the Lord's love for me right then and there, and asked Him to come into my heart."

I know no matter what we will be together as a family, something that I didn't have before—and it will be a large family too, I hope. I could see the Lord in her and her mother's life. Now we have someone else in our lives to carry us on to bigger and better things.

"There will always be things that come into our lives Frank," Mia said, "like trials but we will always know that we are not alone in the trial whatever it is."

This is how I knew Mia was the one. I didn't have to date others to know who is real. This is a love that comes from our heavenly Father that touched our hearts. Both of us will go to the Lord for any and all decisions, large or small. This has been an awesome experience to see how He has even kept us pure from wrongdoing. When we are being tempted we go to prayer and ask Him to help us be strong.

This has caused us to love each other even more. It has a lot of meaning to us to be an example to our children when we have them, as well as to my students, remember they signed a pledge.

You can see again, it is not religion but relationship. Let's go on and see more of what the Lord is going to bring into our lives. We have turned all our plans over to Him as He has done a great job so far.

Mia and I are both agreeable to always put the Lord first in our lives. Now we will try to think of Him before we think of ourselves. There's where the challenge is going to come in, and only time will tell if we are serious about that. I believe we are going to have a strong marriage, as we are already one in our desires.

One of the mothers whose daughter is in my class volunteered to make Mia's wedding gown, as she is a seamstress, and Mia accepted her offer to do that for her. Like I said before, I am not going to restrict anyone from being a part of putting this event together, we are building strong relationships with the people in our lives. This can only get better, and we are being sensitive to anything that might cause any hard feelings.

This is quite different from the background I came from and I am enjoying it. You see, it's not about me anymore. I don't have to protect me. I can be open, that's what a relationship is all about. I am not thinking of the past it is gone forever, only what is present and ahead is important to me now. I want to live it to the fullest, and be open to whatever will build a strong relationship with Mia and the people that have been put into our lives, and I love people.

We talked it over, Mia and I, to not have a sign in our lives that says closed, and we both want to be open to new experiences. This is a danger and we are aware of it to be cautious and be good listeners to those who will advise us.

We talked about never being so busy that we would neglect our own relationship, we will set aside time for just us and our family when we have one.

We are not going to rush into things, we want to savor all of what this event can bring so no date has been set yet, but soon I hope. I am nervous about being a husband to Mia and son to Gertrude. Sometimes we just sit back and watch all that is going on and think of all the blessings from the people who are helping us. Right now we are the recipients of helping hands, but we are also still doing things in our community.

Mia and Gertrude make lunch for all the workers and we sit together and just enjoy getting to know them and their families—who are always welcome to come to the ranch. There is a lot of joy around us; no one talks about things that might cause hard feelings. This in itself is a blessing.

No doubt you are saying it looks like everything is perfect, or we're in some kind of utopia. Nothing is that perfect, but people and families are benefiting from working together—with each other first, and then with my girls who have so much love in them. It just oozes out and spreads over all of us, really it does.

Sometimes Gertrude talks to the wives, to help them with how to strengthen their relationship with their husbands and advice in dealing with their children. This is also part of what they do in their business with handicapped people, sometimes their emotional problems get in the way of dealing with the handicap they have.

As a social studies teacher, I never got this training in college, but I am taking it all in now. We had a class in sociology, you will be surprised what that word entails. The subject takes in all that we have been experiencing thus far. The theme is building relationships.

It's Sunday and off to church with the townspeople. Mia, Gertrude, and I went on our horses in Western wear as did others. We are beginning to fit into the community here. I love singing the hymns, I asked to be part of the worship team and was granted the privilege to do it.

I listen to the message and realize this is an honor I never had growing up, I am gaining a lot of good relationships. Now some of the people we have helped are coming to church, they had never come before.

We rode our horses to get lunch and had a great time with the townspeople who were there, and then Mia's mom left us to go on a ride just the two of us. We are enjoying spending time together and riding over the countryside.

It was time to move forward with the statewide plan to go to the next school and my class wanted to go with us. The principal gave the okay and we sent permission slips home with the students. I scheduled a bus for the students and went to pick up the double horse trailer from Mia's neighbor. It was so gracious of him to offer it to us to use. There were no problems and it was exactly what we had in mind if we were going to buy one ourselves, it was show quality complete with mag wheels. I took it to the ranch and thought I should put both horses in it to see if the two of them would ride together all right, and they did.

The next day after school I went to meet the principal of the school, where the event was to be held, to make the arrangements and assist in any way I could. I also wanted to see if we needed to do anything extra to make this a great success. They had the platform in place and the PA system tested. As I talked to the staff, they told me how excited they were with the possibility of having the same thing happen at their school that we all experienced at mine.

The day had come and all the players were present waiting for us, we were on time of course. Again some of the parents of my class were there. They wanted to show support to both us and their children; this is a life-changing exercise.

I had already decided to give my class an A for the semester, all of them.

We unloaded the two horses and Mia and I rode them to the staging where we faced the people and raised the horses as if to say, "Howdy." The crowd loved it and stood and clapped.

This time we assigned several students to assist us and others will at the next event. The assigned students came and helped us down and led us to the platform holding the horses. As we came to the microphone to welcome everyone, all the people remained standing and applauded.

I told a few stories when all of a sudden a limo pulls up. It's the governor again, but this time he had a lady with him. It turns out to be the mayor of the town we were in. All eyes were on the two of them, and as they came up to the platform, I said lets give them a round of applause. I leaned over to the principal and said, I think it would be appropriate for you to introduce them and sat back down.

There was a lot of sweet-smelling admiration in the air, and all eyes were on all three of the dignitaries as each spoke. They praised me and Mia along with our students and their parents, for what they were hearing and seeing in our town. They also congratulated us on the upcoming wedding. When the last one spoke and sat down, I got up and thanked them for the pleasant words and said, "Now on to the performance."

Just then the client shows up, you know, the veteran. This time all dressed up so beautifully, looking like Elvis Presley. We began by doing some tricks with the horses, some that we had trained them to do. We had them dressed up some too. This was going to be entertaining as well as instructive.

Before we started with the demonstration we had Jake the veteran share his story from his wheelchair in front of the platform. And as he did, Trigger my horse went over to him and rubbed his nose on Jake's arm, you see they were best of pals.

Jake just kept on with his story as he was rubbing Trigger. Jake went on to say that trigger saved his life as well as Mia's horse, Wonder. He told how he was going to take his life, not just because of losing his leg, but also from the trauma of what he went through in battle. "You have a hard time getting over killing someone, you have flashbacks that won't go away. But when I started training with these two friends, referring to the horses, and also Mia and Frank…these are quite the team," he said. "And this couple is from another planet, but gave me a new perspective about all I went through."

He wheeled up to Wonder, and without the help of anyone, he got up on her as we stood by just in case. He had practiced a trick different from the one he did before. So as he had both horses alongside each other, all of a sudden as he rode he stood up on one leg and then jumped up on Trigger landing on the one leg. The crowd roared, then he did the unthinkable and jumped off landing on the ground on one leg, and then got back up on Trigger again. He then got back in the wheelchair, but not before the people applauded.

We then had the children that were there too, who went through therapy, tell how each of them had been helped. They started with thanking the staff and Mia and me for all the care for them, not just the riding, but helping them with their fears and trauma because of the disability. They told of not being able to walk or run before the training, and with that the three of them lined up and ran down the field.

There was a lot of applause and this was better than we had anticipated. The children did that on their own, it was a surprise to us too. Now to put the icing on the cake, my class got up and shared what they all had prepared and nominated one student to read what they wrote together, the rest stood by her.

She told how this has changed their lives to now wanting to contribute something to less fortunate people in their community.

(Applause)

She went on, "We also want to get all we can from our studies and be better students; as they say, charity should start at home."

(More applause)

So we started with our class, and then at home to show our parents how much we love them for what they do for us. We discussed this as a class one day when our teacher had to leave for a meeting with the principal; we elected one of the kids in class to carry on with the lesson. He suggested we talk about relationships with our families first, and each other next. And when the teacher came back to class, he just took a seat and let the one we elected finish out the class. We were blown away to see the respect he had for us.

(Applause)

It's not just the horse therapy that was the start of this, we could see through it that people were being helped and lives were being changed. We saw our friend the veteran who went to war for us and got hurt for us, so we needed to come up close to make a difference in his life too. And now it's about relationship. After that, through the horses working with these people, we then saw the need to help those who can't help themselves. It's still about relationship, that is what our teacher has been teaching us by example. If horses can help people then we should be able to also.

(Applause)

She and the class sat down and I was almost without words to express my feeling. After composing myself, I said it's not about me. I then told my story about being an orphan.

"As an orphan, I was bitter for what life had dealt me. Then one day the staff gave us Bibles and I read how the creator became a man and then gave His life for me. I wanted to have a relationship with Him and asked Him into my heart. Then I decided to be a teacher and make a difference through my life. So, if anyone is to get credit for all that you are witnessing, the credit goes to the Lord Jesus Christ."

(Applause)

"I am so humbled to have such a wonderful life now. No regrets only gratitude for the privilege in being a help to my students, to show them the way. If they choose not to go that way, that's totally up to them. But, I am so proud of them right now; words just don't do justice to what I am feeling. So thanks for sharing this time with us, and you are all invited to Mia's and my wedding next week."

I turned to give recognition to my students and then to my friend Jake the veteran, along with the mayor and governor and of course, Mia.

All applauded again:

The governor spoke to show his appreciation for all who came, and then addressed us as being creditable people to share our lives like we do. The mayor also spoke and said that she will never be the same again. This has been a life-changing event, and it's not going to stop here either.

She then turned to all of us with tears in her eyes and said, "Thank you all for your contribution, and I hope this is the beginning of a strong relationship."

(More applause)

The principal then spoke and said this went beyond his wildest dreams to see lives changed like we just experienced here today.

My thanks go out to each and every one of you for your contribution. I thank you Mia and Frank for being the people you are, I will never forget this day for as long as I live. I am speaking as one of the people in this community not as a principal, and I thank you for the invitation to be at your wedding, I will be there."

I closed out by thanking everyone for coming and then introduced the school band; they were waiting for us to finish so they could play. They played the national anthem and we all stood and saluted. This couldn't have been any better; I felt so close to everyone that day. We just built a bridge between two communities.

The governor waved as he exited and drove off. He said in his speech that this was going to be the start of a great movement statewide if he had anything to say about it.

I was not sure what that meant exactly until some time

later.

We got my class loaded on the bus to go back home, and we loaded Wonder and Trigger into the trailer and all headed home together. This event was even better than the one before, people helping along with the class. We may not have recognized all the ones who were there, but I don't think they minded as this was not about the celebrities or us. We are building bridges where others are tearing them down. I guess we will get better as we go along, hopefully.

Now we have to start thinking about making the preparation for this coming weekend when Mia and I will be one. I am getting so excited thinking that just a year ago I had no thought I would ever be doing events, or getting married. I will never be the same again, and that is beyond my wildest dreams.

We all need love in our lives, and I have been given a large dose of it.

Chapter 6
Getting married to Mia

We are several days away from the special event, but no anxiety just a feeling of excitement as we will have all of our friends with us as well as continue to build relationships with others. I started first with Mia, next with her mom, and then with the people of the community. Now we get to share our lives with all the parties involved. The community, those who have put so much into helping us prepare for this celebration, are still going to be a part of seeing a new relationship emerge.

We are all having such fun, and I get to see Mia in so many different situations. She is such a balanced individual and I am falling in love all over again with her, she is a gift from God without a doubt. She is not controlling, but manages things well and is a joy to be around. I just stand back and watch how she takes challenges in stride and people love her.

The community all went together and gave us an all-expense paid trip to Maui for our honeymoon and even rented car for us. We are beside ourselves, but we felt that we had to allow them to do this; it is going to strengthen that bridge more. We will never forget their kindness, and of course we will be using this as an example to my students too. They will see that when you help people, and when you are in need they will help you.

Oh the lessons we learn in life, they are good if you are a good student and want to learn, they are going to be beneficial too. I think the adage would fit here that says, "You teach others how to treat you." Of course it is by example, this is how that works.

I am, for one, not expecting anything from what I do for

others, that is not my motivation I just love giving back. By that I mean for those who took me in when my parents died. It may not have been exactly the best, but it was a place where I grew up; also those who helped me to be able to go to college.

I will forever be grateful for the example they were to me.

I'm having a hard time sleeping; I am so excited to imagine what this is going to be since I spent all of my life so far being pretty much alone. I don't ever remember cuddling up with my mom or being around a sister, so this teacher is going to be a student for a while. I sure hope I get an "A" for good behavior and learn to always have the greatest respect, in every situation we come to.

I remember a man told me one time that he allowed his wife to make all the small decisions and he would make the large ones; he went on to say that so far there have not been any large ones. No, I am not going to do that one, we will make them together. I may have to make the final decisions on things, but with permission.

Now remember, I had no example from my mom and dad to know how a husband should treat a wife, haven't read any books on the subject of being a good husband either. But I did read the Bible and got some good instruction there about my responsibility. I also picked out from the families of my students where I felt the husband was a good example, to ask advice from them.

One man said that he and his wife still go on dates; he said, "My wife goes to her parents house and I pick her up there to go on a date. She takes the children there for grandma and grandpa to enjoy them, and it feels just like our first date. So keep the fires burning and never take each other for granted, keep the marriage alive, whatever it takes." It was also suggested to always show my appreciation for her, maybe even give her a corsage. In doing this you are showing how special she is to you.

I was actually doing these things somewhat before we were engaged, but now it is to continue throughout our marriage too. I do get that and am looking forward to having the privilege of showing Mia how much I love her, not going overboard but living like a married couple should. And that is always thinking of the other person more than myself.

We continue to get everything just right for our wedding, so years later we will have the memories of what we are experiencing right now.

When we got engaged I asked permission to build a small lake on the property since there was a lot of it. They both agreed, so with the help of the local farmers we dug with dozers and put boulders all around to make it look as natural as possible. The water came from a stream that came in one end and went out the other. There was a landscaper who volunteered to do most of the work, complete with bushes, trees, and grass. All this was done a while back so everything was growing well and looking great. I said to Mia that I would love to have the lake planted with fish and a few ducks. I could help the handicap children learn how to fish, and also feed the ducks.

She didn't have to even think about it before she answered, "Yes, what a great idea."

I told her that I would call the fish and game and arrange for them to do it for us. One of the contractors asked if he might put paths to the lake from the front of the property and also around the lake, so we have almost a park.

An electrical contractor came and put lights around the lake too. It seems that our community has caught on to people helping people. This is something I will never forget for a very long time, and it's all happened since we decided to get married on the ranch. But what is most exciting about what is happening, is now the community has a place to celebrate their anniversaries and just come for a picnic, this is part of building relationships.

The fish arrived along with the ducks someone donated. We tested the lights and they all worked great. Now we are having wild geese coming on the lake too. Someone brought park-type benches to put around the lake, all this just a day before the wedding. That night Mia and I went out and just sat there and admired all the things people had done with us. There was a surprise waiting; you guessed it, a full moon.

It's the day we all have been waiting for, and the time for the ceremony was to be at 10 o'clock. We, at the Milady Ranch were all up early to put the final touches on everything, like dressing up Wonder and Trigger. I had not seen Mia's dress yet or her in it, they say it's bad luck and we sure don't want that.

All of a sudden two buses drove up and it was the two bands from the schools where we had our events. The principals from both schools, and their wives, were with them. Next came the students from the schools. We had anticipated there would be a lot of people and it was fine with both of us.

Mia said, "The more the merrier."

I was all dressed up, and of course Mia was in hiding until the music started. Next came the two mayors and the governor with their wives; their children were on the buses.

Next came the veteran, Jake. Wow, was he looking good, he was dressed up in a western suit with all the trimmings. My best man will be the preacher from the church we attend as the governor wanted to officiate. Mia chose her sister to be her maid of honor; last night was my first time meeting her.

Where are the other ladies who will be with Mia, and where are the ones who will be with the best man? I am going to surprise you! In your wildest dreams you would not guess. Well, you know we are building relationships right? In holding to that, Mia asked the wives of the two principals to be in her party and I asked the two principals to be in mine.

The only thing missing is the two who will be taking hold of the horses when we are off, and now they are here. We got a sidesaddle for Mia for when she rides in with Jake on our horses—remember, Jake is giving Mia away. On signal the band started playing "Tell Me That You Love Me." Then they played," I Love You Truly."

When they finished Mia was ready, so they played the traditional "Here Comes the Bride".

She is stunning and more beautiful than I could imagine. Just before they rode up, the flower girls sprinkled the path with rose petals, they were Mia's sister's girls. They too were beautiful in the dresses their mom made for them.

Now here comes Jake and my bride to be, I just sat there on trigger and admired what I was seeing. I didn't even think about all the people, all I could see was Mia. As the crowd was standing, it was some sight to see the respect that was being given to Mia and Jake. As they got close my horse let out a sound in approval. Mia came close and Jake hugged Mia, then gave me her hand. I slid off Trigger still holding Mia's hand and helped her off Wonder and as I did, two of the students took the horses and brought them to stand next to us.

As we stood there, all of a sudden the band played the national anthem at which time there was a flyover by the armed forces. It was the governor's idea and I have to tell you that at this moment, I broke down. In a moment of time I reflected on where I came from to where I am now. Mia factors into that and she was crying too. I don't think we were the only ones either, this was the most spectacular event I've ever known.

The governor spoke of the joy this couple brought into all of our lives and said, "I can't do enough for them."

He then spoke about the meaning of marriage and the importance of respecting each other. "But for this couple I don't have to say that, as they have been the example to all of us. I have come to admire them and Mia's mom, as well as all of the students here today. This truly has been an extreme pleasure to take part in this fantastic event."

The ladies then sang a beautiful love song, again the love that everyone is showing has penetrated my heart, and Mia's too. The crowd all stood as they were singing.

Afterward, the people sat down and I said my vows to Mia, and she said hers.

My vow:

"My dear Mia, may I never forget the day we were brought together, that wonderful day when you had a flat tire. You then invited me for breakfast and I spent the day learning who you were. Mia, you have twisted our two hearts together and tied them with a bow of love and kindness. I will love you until my time ends and then for eternity. I promise to love you more and more each day. I love you so much for accepting me as I am, and I thank the Lord for bringing me to you."

Mia's vow:

"My dear sweetheart, I love you right now with my whole being. From the first day we met I have loved you. I know that the Lord brought you to me. I asked the Lord that very morning to send to me who He had made for me. Frank, honey, I will always love you. You are a gift from God, and I will thank him always for the time we will have together. Frank, I love you so much and for all you have taught me, you are mine forever. Thanks for accepting me too."

Then the governor said to me, "Do you, Frank, take Mia to be your lawful wedded wife?"

"I will."

"Do you Mia, take Frank to be your lawful wedded husband?"

"I sure do."

Then there was an exchange of rings and he said, "I now pronounce you man and wife, you can kiss the bride."

He then introduced us as Mr. and Mrs.-------

Our horses were taken, and walked behind us as we walked down memory lane. We greeted each person as they exited, lots of hugs and kisses. Was this to be the happiest day of our lives? No, it was just the start.

We had all the guests roam around and make themselves at home while our staff took the chairs and placed them by tables. We also had gifts for everyone who had participated in the festivities.

Everyone commented on the beautiful landscape with the lake and all. These are things we will enjoy for many years.

"Frank," Mia said, "We are husband and wife, how do you feel?"

"Honey, there are no words to describe what I am feeling right now, but I will say, it's like a little piece of heaven to me. Mia, I don't deserve to be this happy, with all the people who are going through terrible things. But at this moment, my love for you is over the top. I just love you so much. We will never have to say, see you tomorrow, I want to be with you for the rest of my life. I finally belong to someone who loves me for whom I am, not just someone in need anymore. I can face tomorrow no matter what with you always by my side, always there to support me, and I will always be there to support you too. That's the best I can come up with right now for what I am feeling. But that being said, it will only get better as time goes on. So ask me that again when all of this newness wears off. What are you feeling right now?"

Mia said, "Sweetheart, I wish that this moment would never wear off. I know what you are saying, and I feel the same way. Yes, we will always be there for each other, I am sure of that. No matter who comes into my life, with the exception of the Lord, you will always come first. We have already built a strong relationship and you are the one I prayed for to have in my life, now it's our lives. We are one. Now let's just mingle with those here."

Music starts:

People started to dance and so did we, Mia and I, to our favorite songs. The governor asked to dance with Mia and I danced with his wife. They are going to be a part of our lives now, I am pretty sure. We both chose one of the students to dance with, to show that we valued them more than just students in my class. We were having a great time and then it was time to eat.

There was a lot of conversation going on, and bridges being built on relationships.

But when they were going to sit Mia and me down, they wanted us to sit on each end of the table. I said, "I am sorry but we will sit at the same end, I will not start our marriage having our friends separate us, as much as we love you."

Mia looked at me and whispered in my ear, "Honey, I love you so much for that, you're right."

At this very moment I reflected back to my earlier life, that little orphan boy who didn't have much love shown to him. And now all these people here are showing so much love to both of us, and to Gertrude too. It was time for the best man to speak so he got up, clicked his glass.

He said, "I want to propose a toast—To a couple whose lives have been so giving to all of us, they will forever be in our hearts and minds. I will never forget them and will try to always use their example. May God bless what ever He puts into their hearts."

There was a loud AMEN by all as they stood with their glasses high.

It was time to say goodbye and the first one to go was the governor and his family. Mia and I had changed into our going away clothes. As they were leaving, we got on our horses and escorted them out of town. When we came back our luggage was all put into the car and we were escorted out of town. We drove to my house as the plane didn't leave until the next morning. So this was a time to just be alone and relax before going on our trip. Before we left Mia and I told Gertrude goodbye and thanked her for all she has done. I thanked her for raising such a wonderful daughter, and thanked her also for accepting me as her son. We got a little emotional at this point and embraced in a family hug.

We took all the gifts from the car into the house.

I said, "Can we leave them unpacked until we get back, would that be all right?"

"Yes" she said, "that way we can spend more time together."

After we did that, I told Mia I had a present for her and handed it to her. She opened it, and it was a plaque with my pledge to remain pure until marriage. I told her I had made that commitment when I went to college, and though there were many times I could have broken my pledge, I never did. Mia said I don't have a plaque to give you but I too saved myself for such a time as this. With that she flew into my arms and we hugged for the longest time.

I stopped and said, "I want to give the Lord thanks for putting us together right now. I love you my lady. "

After both of us prayed, a thought came to me, "Mia, can I share what the Lord just put on my heart as we prayed?"

"Yes, please do."

"This is going to be by permission only, you will have to agree to it."

"Okay, what is it? I am all ears."

"I want to know if we might wait to have relations and take our time at it. I want to show to you that I married you for more than sex. I want it to be ever so very special and I want to build a relationship based on our love for each other, can we do that?"

Mia looked at me and said, "I was wondering what we would do after being married, and I have to say yes, I would love that. I want to take our time too, but where did you come from, you are not a normal guy. I not only admire you as my husband but respect you as a person and see you as that very special person too, you are truly a gift from the Lord."

I talked to some of the husbands and they knew fellows that rushed into consummating their marriage and spoiled the marriage. The wife never forgot it and it wrecked what could have been a great relationship. One group of fellows said, "The only reason you get married is to have sex, otherwise you wouldn't need to."

I said, "What if your wife gets an illness and you can't have sex, what then, do you throw her away?"

"No" I said, "it must be based on love and respect. So you see why the Lord laid that on my heart, sweetheart?"

Mia's response was, "I think Maui is going to be a memorable time that we will never forget."

"I just want to hold you and get those hugs I didn't get growing up."

Mia said, "This is going to be more than a physical union, a spiritual one as well, right?"

"Yes."

Chapter 7
Honeymoon in Maui

*I*t was the following morning and time to get to the airport to catch our flight to Maui. We are both very excited and called for our ride to pick us up; it was the principal that asked to do this the day before. He had picked up a few things as it was going to be a long flight. Coffee, which we don't usually drink, but it was from Star—a special brew just for us. He also gave us some treats to hold us over.

We are now aboard and ready to take off; alone again and on our way to a new adventure. All the brochures we saw were beautiful, and had a lot of side things to see and do—whale watching, a submarine tour.

We checked into our suite by the ocean, and the sun was going down. Both of us stopped what we were doing and went down to sit on the sand and enjoy the sunset. I can't tell you what it looked like; it took our breath away. We just sat there and would you believe, we fell asleep in each other's arms! There was no one around, so this became our private beach.

Mia has her camera and we are taking a lot of pictures to remember this special time—we were given an all expense paid trip by Mia's community. I guess the old adage still holds true, "When you give, it comes back to you tenfold."

We decide to head for bed, and when Mia turned down the blankets there were silk sheets on the bed. I have never slept in anything like this before. The next morning we got up to a sunny bright day, and made plans to get the car that was rented for us and see the city.

This is the most amazing place on earth. We drove

taking turns at the wheel so we could get the most from our experience. We saw great open spaces and all kinds of wild game; and the greenest grass I have ever seen, coupled with the ocean in the background.

We are going on the submarine tomorrow to see all the underwater creatures. More than anything, Mia and I are elated and seeing each other in new light, I thank the Lord all the time for His graciousness to bring us together.

I am watching her react to people and I have to tell you, she puts me to shame. We have even made new friends that we will contact later. Mia is truly a help to broaden our range of friends, I am so looking forward to doing things together with the people we have met.

We enjoy walking the beach after dinner, sometimes formal and sometimes not. We enjoy the beach cafes the most. It's kind of interesting that I am a city guy and Mia is a country girl. Mia is just like a kid, kicking water at me and running away so I can catch her. She is full of fun and shows me that she is going to make a great mother.

I know there will be challenges in the future, and I am so thankful we both look to the Lord already for things we don't understand. This will be our mindset for the rest of our lives. We just sit and hold each other as we watch all that goes on around us. I will always remember this time that was given to us and the friends who made this experience possible.

We went on the excursion to the bottom of the sea today and took all kinds of pictures to share with our friends.

Now we are learning to ride the waves, such fun. Tomorrow we will go see the volcano and look inside it, something I can share with my students when we return home. But in all that we do, we are not neglecting each other's needs.

We don't think about what we can do for one other, we just do it. We're becoming one and always think of the other person before me or us.

We found a group on the beach who loves to play hymns and we join them, they are glad to have us. I love singing and have a great range in my voice. Mia has a beautiful voice too. We were singing "This little light of mine, I'm going to let it shine."

We are learning to share our faith more, which is new to me, but it makes a lot of sense and every place we go it seems that people are attracted to us.

Both Mia and I love people, Mia because of her desire to help people and I because of being isolated during my time as an orphan. It seems that no matter where we go we want to not only fit in, but to be of help also.

We are enjoying going on bus tours and interacting with people, it's a lot of fun and I don't want it to stop. In my wildest dreams I would never thought it would be as peaceful as it was beautiful. Our time here is almost up; it is a memory we will always cherish, along with how we first began as husband and wife. It may even carry us through hard times to be able to reflect on this adventure.

You might be saying that I am putting too much on this time, but you would have to have lived as I did to understand why I said that. We have grown in so many ways, more in love for sure. It has gone from wanting to share a life with someone to absolutely surrendering ourselves to one other. We have both lived a single life, and now it's about adjusting to having someone else to think about. We are making this adjustment very well, couldn't think about being apart ever again.

We are getting packed to return home now and we're both being very quiet. We really don't want to leave here and this will always be our special place to remember. In years to come we will make this a place to come to and spend some time again, remembering this is where we started our lives together.

Reading the account of our lives, it seems like everything is perfect which is far from the truth, I just haven't gone into the negatives. It's never with Mia and I however, just life, you know!

As for Mia and I, there has never been a single word of regret for anything, and it is because we talked everything over together first. Yes, I had to give up on some things and so did Mia, but things come into everyone's life to rattle their well-being. I am not going to say that at times it is something we had to go around and not let it destroy us. Whenever you deal with people there will most always be something to cause concern, but both of us have gone past all that to have the best possible time of our lives.

We are back home now and time to get back to living the life that has been picked out for us. Neither of us have any regrets and are moving forward to continue what we started.

We had a dinner with Mom and she said that she wanted to talk to us about redoing the guesthouse for her to live in, and give Mia and I the family house. I said not in your wildest dreams, I am not going to allow that to happen. "Well, what are you suggesting then?" Mom said?

"I want to build a house for me and Mia, if you would let me do that. I want you to be able to stay in your house and as for the guesthouse, we can still use it for honored guests."

I then turned to Mia and said, "Honey, I am sorry not to have mentioned a plan I had before this but Mom sprung this on us, and Mom I just love you for the offer, you are so gracious. Mia, what do you think about what I proposed, would you be willing to do that if Mom gives us an okay?"

"Sweetheart, I love the idea, let's do that if Mom agrees, what do you think Mom?"

"I think it is a great idea, I just put myself in your shoes for a minute and that's exactly what I would have done if in the same circumstance. Yes, of course, but where will you build?"

I said, "Mia, Mom, do you have any ideas for the best place? I have not thought that far ahead. "

"I do want to live on this property as I want us to be a close family always."

Mia said, "This is the greatest idea you've had yet and I love you so much," and with that Mia got up and gave me a big hug. And then Mom came over too and I got another one from her.

Mia said, "Even though we haven't had a chance to talk about it before, it's all right".

"Mom, I want to make something very clear, I so appreciate your offer, but I am thinking ahead when we have children. It would be better to enjoy them apart from them living in your house, but be close so they could run over to grandma's house." Both ladies agreed and Mom thanked me for the consideration.

"I wanted you to have your privacy," I said. "And who knows, you might fall in love and have a husband again someday."

We talked about where to build it and I suggested it should not be too close to the lake for safety reasons, and the ladies agreed.

"I am so excited," I said, "to think of my upbringing and now we're talking about raising a family. I think Mia and I will be looking over the ranch for the best place to build our house."

Then we can come back together to finalize the plans, thank you so much Mother. I've been waiting a long time to say that, too."

People got word that we were thinking of building a house on the ranch property. Right away an architect was contacting me and wanted to assist us in making a plan. We set a time to meet and go over what we are thinking about the house. In the meantime Mia and I went over what each of us wanted, that took some discussion before we ever met with Jim the architect, to get his opinion.

It's time to get back to school for me and some very excited students, they wanted details having never been in Maui.

"Well, first I have to tell you that none of this would have happened if it weren't for your generosity to volunteer to help the community. I owe you a lot of gratitude; I will always be indebted to you all. This has been a great lesson for all of us; I will never forget it."

"So where are you in your lessons since I've been gone, class? Jennifer, why don't you tell me."

"We studied how America began and the suffering they endured because England wanted to invade the Americas. We saw how the Indians responded to the early settlers and taught them how to live off the land. It was fantastic how they got along, this is not what we're told."

" So where did the fighting start, and why do they have to live on reservations? These are good questions and we will finish up that story. I had these same questions growing up and I got the encyclopedia out to find out the why. Now you have Google, a great place to find answers to hard questions. Tomorrow we will get the answer, but it's your homework tonight to look it up. "

"In the meantime I will share what we experienced in Maui. We were given a fancy hotel to stay in overlooking the ocean. It was right on the beach, so we went and sat on it to watch the sunset. It was very romantic and we fell asleep as the sun went away.

"The next days we toured the island to see all the wild game and saw these beautiful birds with long legs, I think they call them flamingos. There were a lot of them among the glorious flowers; I can still see them and smell the flowers, too. Then we hiked up the mountain to see the volcano, here are some pictures of our experiences. I'll put them up on the screen."

I did this for my class to reward them for making this time possible through their assistance in the communities where we helped the people who needed it. I told the class that both Mia and I wished they could have been there to witness this awesome experience.

I had pictures that we took from the submarine of all kinds of fish with all the colors imaginable. With that the whole class got up and huddled around just like a family would, which they are, that's how I feel about them.

This makes for a great learning tool, I don't have a class out of control anymore. It's really not about control, though, it's about relationship. The principal got wind of what we were doing in class and came to watch. Then he asked if we might do that for the student body. "What a great idea! Yes, and can I invite Mia to come too?" The principal said of course. I thought this would be a great opportunity to thank the whole school. Another surprise came when all the parents were also invited.

What happened next blew me away because the families from Mia's town asked permission to come, and the principal agreed. The local police force was going to be there too. They said they wanted to honor the school for their contribution to show what happens when people care.

Mia should be a professional photographer as she was clicking all the time and everywhere we went.

Well, the time arrived and everyone was present. The school wanted to have a great event, so out came the orchestra and flag corps.

The principal introduced the chief of police first and he honored our school with a plaque for excellence and gave a speech.

He said, "This school has exemplified what it means to teach more than reading, writing, and arithmetic; it has taught something more valuable than that. It has taught that when we give, it comes back a hundredfold. You have shown that you love country and community too. It is more than Mia and Frank, though it started with them. But you all have taken it to a new level. We are drug-free now and you have made our job so much easier, so all of you give a big hand for each other."

After all the speeches, including ones from the mayor and governor, and from the two principals from the two cities plus the awards, it was time to see the videos of Mia and me.

To our surprise, after the videos, a travel agent presented to us an all-expense paid trip next year for our wedding anniversary.

The travel agent then did the unthinkable. He first thanked us for showing the video, and then the school's faculty and students for all the work they have done in the community. He then turned to the principals, mayor, and governor to thank them for their part and said this would not have happened without all their efforts. After this, he offered to anyone who wanted to go to Maui a 50% discount. "You can come to my office and pick out a date. This is my contribution to show my appreciation to all of you who have helped make this a great community. A big round of applause for all who took part to make this a momentous occasion. And again, thank you Mia and Frank for making this all possible."

This has pulled everyone together as a community and there was talk of all going together. A committee was established who would put all this together, but first they had to ask permission of us. We talked it over and told the committee that we would consider it an honor to be with everyone. We had a whole year to make plans, and I said to Mia, I have more family now and it's getting bigger all the time. Mia was overwhelmed with great expectations of what that would entail.

I told her not to worry and there's nothing that would ever get in the way of our own family's activities, but think about our children and the example we are going to be showing. Mia agreed and sealed it with a hug, I loved that.

Chapter 8
Getting ready to build

$\mathcal{A}$ll the excitement has died down now and we are talking about going forward with our plans. Mia and I went all over the property checking out a suitable spot for the new house, and we decided to put it on the other side of the lake. Now we have to decide what we want in the house, and then I will have the plans drawn up. When I was going to college, I had to pay for my rent and food so I worked in construction. I am somewhat familiar with how to build a house and am looking forward to doing most of the work.

I have been considering getting a teaching job in Sky View, the town closest to where our ranch is. I say ours because I have been made a partner with Mia and Gertrude, it's ours now. They want me to take care of the workers so they can concentrate on the horse therapy part of the business. Anyway, it works out better as the guys would rather have a man in charge giving orders, which I don't necessarily agree with. I will take this as my part of the job at the ranch, and of course will enjoy working with the guys too. I have already gotten familiar with how things were done before, so will not change anything right away. If I can see a better way as I go then I'll mention it to the gals first, after all this is their livelihood we are talking about.

I went to the superintendent of schools in Sky View to talk over what I had planned and see if there might be an opening to teach in one of the schools in town. I was told there was going to be an opening after summer break in the middle school and it would be right down my alley, it is a Social Studies class. I told him this is great news as it's a long drive every day otherwise, for me to continue where I am teaching now.

Bill, the superintendent asked me to call him and said he was happy that I considered being a part of their school system. He went on to say he was aware of what I had already been doing in the town and hoped I would continue encouraging that. I said it was my intention and thanked him for the encouragement.

I then went to my school and talked to Henry, the principal, about my plan to change schools.

His reply was, "I was wondering when you would do this, but I do understand. You will go with my blessings as you have definitely changed my life for the better. I invite you to be a part of this school in whatever you can do to keep up the momentum in the changes that have taken place."

I assured him that I would try to include what we do in Sky View with this school too.

Now Mia and I have to decide on how many bedrooms and bathrooms we want in our new house before we go to the architect. I made a sketch of a floor plan and both of us wanted the same things. We started out with a four bedroom/four bath, one bath off of the kitchen, one for two bedrooms, and one bath for the master bedroom. That will leave one for the hallway for anyone to use. I now have something to put in the website I found to make us a blueprint. It looks like it's going to be a large house. The downstairs will be for a living room, formal dinning room, and a kitchen.

School is about to start, we have one more week and I wanted to spend it with Mia and my class. I asked Mia if she felt it was a good plan, and she immediately said it is a great idea. She said how do you come up with these things, Frank? I said I just want to cement our relationship since I am not going to be their teacher next semester. I want them to feel that they can come to us at any time for advice or just to hang out, or maybe they might like to work for us.

What I've been witnessing is a change in attitude with the heads of the schools. They are for the people and take their job seriously, not leaning on their titles but being real people. As a result, I will back them to the hilt.

We invited my class to come and join us in a backcountry trip with the horses, we'll have a wagon with food and cooking utensils and other things we may need. They are to bring a tent and any camping gear they want. We will see wild game and do some trapping, maybe even take down a deer as I have a deer tag to use. This way we will have fresh meat and I will teach them how to do this. I learned how to hunt from a fellow I used to go hunting with when I was in college. This was after I was with the man that wanted to adopt me.

The kids were on time and excited about doing this. Mia will take care of the girls and I will take the boys, meaning the boys and girls will be encouraged to be ladies and gentlemen. I don't anticipate any problems as we took care of that in the classroom some time ago. They learned to have respect for each other and we witnessed it. We will have to teach some of them how to be out in the wilderness. Some have never been camping let alone being out where human life is not present, just us and the animals. Of course we will be fishing too, I got fishing poles from the bait shop, enough for each of the kids. So this is going to be an exciting venture.

I don't think they're going to get homesick because of our love for them, and they know it. They have seen us through all kinds of situations and how we handle things, they have confidence in our leadership.

We said goodbye to Mom and off we went to see how they would follow instructions. We both were blown away as the kids went beyond our expectations; they rode three abreast, perfect. When someone had to go to the bathroom there was a lot of respect shown. First day was good and we ate the things we brought.

We also had some help with everything as one of the ranch hands went with us; he was an experienced backwoods guy and a good cook. He didn't do all of it as Mia was a great cook also. We ate high off the hog, well at least bacon for breakfast. I had taken tables but no one wanted to eat at the tables, wanted to rough it they said. We had given them a wilderness kit, which included a shovel to dig a hole when they use the bathroom. I felt this was not going to be the last trip we would do together.

These kids were funny. You know they were just starting into their teens but we got them before all the teen problems, and we looked to have them in our lives even when they go off to their careers. We knew this trip was going to build strong relationships and the parents were very cooperative, we didn't have to convince them of its importance and they trusted us.

At night we would sit around the fire, tell stories, and sing camp songs. Some of the kids had brought their instruments with them as we encouraged them to do that. They didn't want to go to bed, and neither did Mia and I. After the kids did go to bed, we just sat around the fire and held each other with a blanket and fell asleep.

I can't wait to have our own family to do this with, and we will.

Morning came and I had one of those triangles that make noise to let them know it's time for breakfast. Mia did the cooking this time and made camp biscuits and gravy, and they were good. Some were a little slow getting up, so I told them I would eat their biscuits if they didn't hurry. That did it, up they came, "You have biscuits?" they would ask. We always showed a sense of humor, after all this was to be a great time, and it was.

But I have to tell you this is because we had already built a relationship before this, that's what it is about. We are family and out for a good time together.

One time when I was at a Bible camp as a counselor for the older boys, I had gone on a hike up in the snow with them. Of course all of our shoes got extremely wet, so as we came back to camp, some put their shoes by the potbelly stove to dry. I didn't go up to the cabin, instead had some hot coffee to warm up with. Well, one of the boys in my cabin decided to put my bunk and belongings up in the rafters as a joke.

I had an informer come down and tell me this and

instead of getting mad, knowing who was behind it and that he had put his shoes by the fire to dry, I took one of the shoes and hid it. He came down to check on them and discovered one shoe was missing,

"Where is my other shoe?"

"Oh," I said, "was that your shoe?"

He said it was, and I told him that it wasn't getting dry outside of the stove so I threw it into the fire.

"But, I can get it out if you run and get my stuff out of the rafters."

My informant told me the stuff was down, so I went and fetched the hidden shoe. When he came back I gave him the shoe and said that I did such a good job getting it out, that it's in the same condition as it was when I threw it into the fire—in other words, still wet.

Sense of humor is what that was about. I was there to have fun too, it's important to build relationships. Sometime later I saw him again, now a little older, and he told me he never forgot the example of not getting mad.

So now I am ready for my class to pull something to have fun, maybe a frog in my knapsack, or a snake. I still have an informer to help with that, someone once said, "I don't get mad, I get even." Mia is up for this too, she is fun-loving and pulls things on me at times.

One time she made a sandwich for me to take to school before we were married. I opened it at lunchtime and started to eat it, only to discover she had put the picture of the meat in with the ham. They used to put the picture of what kind of meat was in the package; she put a note in that said, "I love you." I just love her for the childish things she does.

As we sat by the fire roasting marshmallows, I reminisced about when I was their age as an orphan and how I dreamed about a time like this. One of the children asked me to share what it was like being raised as an orphan. I said I didn't know if I want to share that. They kept insisting and I said that it is sometimes very painful to talk about.

"I will tell you, but I might have to stop." I said that

what I am about to share with you, Mia hasn't even heard. I think it will benefit you, however, as you go home and think about what I am going to tell you.

"I was two years old when my parents died, my mom first at birth and my dad two years later, and no one wanted to take me. I was sent to an orphanage where I was to spend most of my life. I never went to Disneyland or fishing with my dad; never had a hug from my mom, and no kind words were ever spoken that I can remember. Sometimes, for no reason, I would get a belt across my backside. We didn't get to play outside except on special occasions. Love was a word that I didn't know the meaning of. I was grateful for a place to live and food to eat, but heard stories of children with families and the fun they had growing up, things I never experienced but wanted."

I broke down at the memories, and said, "I can't go on with my story because of what happened to me. I am sorry for breaking down, but it is still so painful to me." Some of the kids came close and were crying too.

At this point Mia came close and hugged me. "I have to tell you what happened to bring me out of this horrible situation."

"When I was your age I had already found someone who did love me. I read in the Bible that Jesus Christ loved me and died for me. From that time on I wanted to bring love into the lives of others less fortunate than me. Now you are getting to know why I do the things I do. I was also given a wonderful wife, Mia, from the Lord; again He showed me His love.

I hope you all can see how much He loves you too. Let the Lord pour His blessings on you, as He has on us, by asking Him to come into your hearts. Let me go on to tell you what happened when I was fifteen years old. A man wanted to adopt me, and as they were going through the necessary paperwork, they allowed me to live with him. He taught me skills in woodwork, taught me how to fish, also many other things about life in general that I was missing out on. One day he got really sick and went to the hospital, but never came out again. He had children who took care of the burial and allowed me to stay in the house. I was now seventeen so I never had to go back to the orphanage. I was also in sports and finished high school with a full scholarship.

I wanted to be a teacher to make a difference. You all know the rest of the story, but thank you for asking me to share my life with you. I will ever be grateful for a life that helped me to see the Lord; maybe if I hadn't been in the situation I was in, I may never have found the Lord or knew His love for me.

I have forgiven those who abused me, and one day I will never remember anything about those things. Let's not go to bed with those negative thoughts, let's sing some songs as the fire dies down. When you are in a quiet places think about the one who died for you too, and ask Him to come into your hearts. That would make all that I went through worthwhile. I am really getting to know you, you young people are the love of our lives and I hope we will always enjoy each other."

Mia and I stayed by the fire and sent the kids to bed. We had our blanket and just held each other.

Mia said honey, "I love you so much at this very moment." This time we didn't fall asleep, just talked about our lives together.

Mia was still thinking about the story I told the kids. "I am so sorry for what you had to go through."

As I wiped the tears from her eyes, I said "All this would not have happened if I hadn't gone through those things, our lives are not in our hands. If I had to go through this to find you, it makes it all worth it. I love you Mia, so very much as you have accepted me just as I am. I mention my time as a child a lot, only because I am so grateful for what I have now. I think of my roots and what has grown out of it. It's a beautiful life that came out of such a horrible beginnings. That is why I mention the Lord so much, as He did it."

The following day we get to see some deer, rabbits, and geese, things these children have never seen up close before. We are seeing them in their natural surroundings. I didn't feel like killing a deer, so instead we went fishing. It was fun to watch them get so excited when they got a fish on the line, so we had fish for dinner that night.

The children are all learning to cook outdoors and taking turns. In the meantime Mia and I are taking care of the horses. We are close to snow country, and we prepared for that and took skis and warm gear in the case the kids didn't bring any. This is another experience for them, skiing.

It's the third day and we are around the fire, Mia asked what each one wanted to do in their lives and they were really open to tell us. Mia was taking notes so we could help steer them in the right direction. I said this is going to be the last day to go exploring as it's time to start back home. They did not want this time to stop; never a complaint, no homesickness, just a great time to get close.

We are close, let me tell you. They told of their fears and some real problems with home situations. They were getting great help from Mia, as this is what she does to help the handicap people. Mia broke in and asked how many went to bed last night and thought about what Frank asked them to do. "I mean to consider the Lord and ask him to come into your hearts, how many did?"

Quite a few raised their hands and Mia said, "We will now thank the Lord." I prayed, and it was truly a time to give thanks.

I noted down the hands that went up so later I could help them grow, we may even have them in our Bible studies.

We are on our way home singing most of the way, and cutting up some too. We are a happy bunch with many stories to tell. There was a lot of respect shown to each other, a real pleasure to witness. The boys would help the girls with putting on the saddles and help them on sometimes.

The parents were at the ranch when we got there, but the children still had to bed down the horses as part of their responsibility. The parents reported later that the children were really making some good choices and showed a lot more consideration.

Children are our heritage, our future, and can grow into great companions and adults. They reflect us as we teach and direct them. When we build a good relationship with them they will always be in our lives as those special people that love us. I can't wait until we have ours, and I am going to take my own advice.

I watched a mother with six children one time when I was still single, and witnessed how she disciplined them. All the children were in the house and their mom was cooking and baking cookies. A fight broke out and instead of sending them to their rooms or hollering at them, which I was ready for, she did the unthinkable. She said to the one causing the problem to come help her with the cookies; it was over and peace was restored. That made an impression on me that I will always remember. She was special, a meek and quiet spirit, which is a great price to the Lord, He says.

Chapter 9

More new adventures and opportunities

*T*oday is a new chapter in our lives, I will meet my new class at the school in Sky View and Mia is back working with the horses. She has new patients since all the publicity we got over the last two events. People are aware of the value of horse therapy more now, and want to test it out to see if it will be beneficial for them too. As this business grows, I can see a future in being more of a part of it while using my teaching skills. I love seeing children grow in their understanding of the world we live in.

My last class took to it like a duck to water and were eager to learn more, but not at first. What made the difference? I will say that I had to be excited about the subject myself, to show this was not just another boring subject they are forced to take.

I learned this from the man that almost adopted me. When he would share life experiences with me, I could tell that he was passionate about what he was sharing. Sometimes he would break into tears, I lived the experience right along with him, so this is how I teach now.

You can see now the method I use works, it's not about getting a certain grade, but being excited about the subject you are studying. I am excited to teach, or rather bring the students into the subject along with me. The subject becomes alive and an adventure to excite and expand the mind to want to experience it more themselves. All eyes are on me, and though we have a book to study from, it can just be like words on a page. But when you give it life, it is different now.

So let's see how this works with my new class, as this is

a required class they have to take. I will borrow from a Social Studies teacher I knew. He was teaching on the civil war, and came to class with the uniform they wore complete with gun belt and rifle. He put himself into the subject and the class got into it too.

Along with the subject, I throw in some building blocks for life. For example, I share that there are no limitations to what you can do only those we put on ourselves.

I was taught this by the man who wanted to adopt me, he also taught me this principle: that someone has done it, it is possible to do, I can do it! I also learned from him that how you do anything is how you do everything. Though we were only together for a short time, he taught me a lot about life

I came early to school to greet the faculty and find my classroom. After I was prepared for my new class coming in, I went and had coffee with some of the teachers. They let me in on some of the problem students, as they had them in their class too. I thanked them for letting me know. Now I can see this is going to start out with a challenge so before the class came in, I had a word of prayer and was still praying when some came in.

They apologized for disturbing me and I said that's all right, I like doing this before starting my day and I didn't get to before coming this morning. I said we should never be so busy that we forget to pray for guidance for the day.

I stood by the door and greeted each one as they came in, then went to the blackboard to introduce myself to the class, and write my name up there. "I have name tags for you all to wear so I can get to know you personally. Most will make a chart by the desk you sit in, but that is not what I do. I will pass them out now and ask the person in front to use the black felt pen and then pass it to the one behind you."

"We are going to share today and get to know each other, and find out about some of your interests. I just took my last class on a trip into the backcountry and we went on horses.

My wife and I own a horse and cattle ranch outside of

town and at some point, I will invite you to come and witness what we do. How many would like to do that?" I asked, and all of their hands went up."

"We also do horse therapy on the ranch, how many know what that is." Just a few raised their hands.

I said, "Sally, what do you know about horse therapy? She said that one of her cousins was born with birth defects, and his mom and dad found a place that did this kind of thing when he was four years old. He was able to function so much better after some time, and now he goes just to ride the horses.

One of the boys raised his hand.

"Yes, Jack?"

"Well, I heard that you started a community project with your other class last year, can you tell us something about that?"

"To start with Jack, I want to thank you for showing respect to the class in raising your hand to ask your question."

"I will give just a little of what happened last year, and it was really a surprise to me. I just made a suggestion, and the school principal took it from there. And yes, we started a community project. Your principal has encouraged me to do that here too, and guess what? You all will be a part of it, but more on that later.

First I want you to know how I grade you in my class, it's different from what you have been used to. I don't make you do homework, we will be doing that in class. You wear your name tags and I observe how you participate in class, and your manners towards your fellow students and me; also some of the activities we will be doing together. I have been given full authority to do this by your superintendent of schools.

Homework has its place, but what I do has proven more successful. I will tell you this, my last class where I used this method got all As for the whole semester.

I believe learning should be fun rather than just a passing grade. You could do the test and pass it just memorizing the subject and never know how or where to use it in real life. What I will be teaching you will take you into and through life. Are you ready to get started?" (Bell ring)

"Don't forget to wear your name tag tomorrow, it is part of how I will be grading you."

The next day comes and the students are all wearing their name tags with an eagerness to learn more from what I will share with them. I was able to break into their world and I want to share mine with them. We want solid students whose minds are open to good things, this is where I start before going into controversy over this war and that. Sometimes we have to cleanse our mind before taking in new thoughts. Sometimes we mimic what we hear, but I want my students to have thought based on fact and not just the media's view on everything.

"Today, class, we are going to discuss what your desires are. You are a year away from high school where you will be asked to plan your future and select classes in preparation for college. Let's start from the back of the room, Betty, would you please start us off?"

"I would like to do that," she said. "I have talked this over with my parents and they want me to choose to be a doctor."

"Well, Sally is this what you want?"

"No, I want to be a veterinarian, I love animals."

"Thank you Betty, I will make a note of that."

What she didn't know is that I will have Mia walk her through what it takes and if she still wants to be that, we will work with her. This to me is going the next mile as a teacher.

"Who is next? Henry, what is it you have thought about?"

"I thought about it, and I want to be a professional football player."

"Good," I said, "that means keeping your grades up, I will talk to the coach here and see if he can help with that.

My thoughts are, it is here that we start preparing you for the next step in your future. I want you all to know that I and the staff are interested in your future, and this is one way to prove it. You are the next generation of Americans to help bring us to be the best that we can be as a nation.

I am counting on you, just as your parents and friends are counting on us to do our best in teaching you, to be the best you can be. I am committed in doing that very thing to the best of my ability. I am spending time right now with you before I interject anything else, agreed? I will be listening to you to do my best to direct you in your future."

The whole class applauded, from that I knew we had their attention. I am not writing a handbook for teaching, I just want results. Not just "A" students, but honest, thinking people that go on facts, not hearsay. I believe we have them, but it's going to make problems when around people who are not on that same page.

There's a PTA meeting tonight and I am encouraged to attend by the principal who asked if I could make it. I called Mia and told her about the meeting, she said we will have dinner early then,

"And can I go too?"

"Yes, of course, I don't see a problem with that."

Mom made my favorite dinner, chicken and dumplings and all that goes with it.

Mia and I saddled up Wonder and Trigger and rode to the school. We were there early to greet all the parents who came. The agenda was special events to do this year; that was right up our alley so I went prepared. The chairman opened by introducing us into the group, and me as the new teacher to the school.

Someone said, "I see you rode your horses into town."

Mia said, " We'd been neglecting them a little and wanted to show our consideration to them. You see," she went on, "in our line of work doing horse therapy, it's important to let them know they are important to us."

The chairman broke in by saying they'd heard a lot

about what we were doing in other towns with them. He then asked the group if they would like Frank and Mia to consider doing that here, raise your hand if so. All the hands went up, and I said that we had talked it over already and are prepared to do that here too.

"Just a minute, excuse me, I will be right back." I went out and got Trigger and brought him into the classroom. I introduced him to everyone, and then asked if he (Trigger) would like to be in a school activity like we did before. We waited, and then Trigger lifted up one leg and shook his head in agreement.

"Thank you Trigger, you are the best but don't tell Wonder I said that," and I took him out.

The whole group applauded. When I came back they wanted to know why I did that, I said you may not know this but horses are very smart and I wanted for Trigger to show you that, and agree with doing this. There were ranchers there who had horses and shared some with the group. I said as you can see, our horses are the key to bringing people help that no one else can give.

There are two things that stand out, Mia said about them, love and relationship. It works and you just witnessed how Trigger responded to Frank, those two are inseparable.

We moved on and the parents directed their questions to me about what their children shared with them. They said they'd never witnessed their children being so excited about going to school. "So tell us Frank, what is your secret?"

I said, "it's what you witnessed when I brought in my Trigger, I don't refer to him as a horse, but by his name. I teach this same way, and that is by respect and relationship. The first day is the most crucial time; I learned this when I was a counselor at a youth camp—that the first day was the key to letting the children know who you are and what's expected of them."

"Well," one parent said, "you sure did that. My kids said that you don't give homework, is that right?"

"Yes, it is. If we can't get it into their minds in class, then no amount of reading will make a difference. I shared this with the superintendent before he hired me, and he was eager to see the results. I told the class that my last class all got an "A" for the semester doing what I taught, and that is relationship and respect; that's what I teach along with the subject. This is what will carry them through life to give them the greatest success."

The parents were blown away and you could see their excitement too. One said, "I wish you were my teacher when I went to school, I hated school."

"I am sorry for that, but you are going to see even more, I promise."

"I am asking each student what they would like to do in life, not what someone else wants them to do. I am writing that down and Mia and I will be talking to you, the parents, to help frame their future. That is if this is all right with you. For example, one student wants to be a veterinarian, so Mia will bring her to the ranch and see how she does with the animals; we have a horse and cattle ranch."

"If Mia thinks she has what it takes, we can then see about a scholarship to make this happen. In the meantime, we will hire her to help with our livestock. We can also work with the local veterinarian. We will do what we can and find others for what we don't have expertise in. My role as a teacher doesn't stop at the classroom door."

"If you are in agreement with this raise your hand," the chairman said. Again all hands went up, someone said, "This is incredible, no one has ever had such commitment like this."

I asked to be able to speak to all the parents in the school as many have not come. The subject will be respect and relationship, the greatest tool for learning in school and in life. "Can we do this for the student body's families?"

The chairman asked for a show of hands, again all went up.

Some had questions like, "Can we bring our friends?" Chairman, "does anyone object?" No one did. So here we go again, I can just imagine what may happen with this.

One of the mothers raised her hand and the chairman gave her audience. "Frank, may I ask you where you learned this."

"Yes, you may. Do you want the short story, or the long one, how much time do you have?"

The chairman broke in and said, "since we are getting to know you, take all the time you need."

"Well, to start with, you will not find this in a study guide it's about how I grew up in an orphanage. There was no respect shown or relationship, at least where I was. In my early teens I read in the Bible that someone loved me and died for me, a sinner.

Respect and relationship is what this person wanted, He said if I would accept Him I would become His son. I grew up not having a mother or a dad. I accepted Him into my heart, and then had a father who showed love to me. Shortly after that a man wanted to adopt me and as they were getting the paperwork finished, I was allowed to live with him. He taught me to always think of the others before I thought of myself. (Respect) Then he taught me how to fish and hunt. (Relationship)

He got sick and went to the hospital but never came out. He had children, so they took care of the funeral and allowed me to stay in the house. I was in high school and was in sports, and as a result I won a full scholarship, all I had to do was pay for food and necessaries as I stayed in the house all through college. My adopted dad, before he died, taught me that how you do anything is how you do everything; there are no limitations in life only those you put on yourselves. Also someone has done it, it is possible to do, you can do it.

These are building blocks for life, and you may have all the education in the world but without these things you won't get very far. You can build relationship in a moment of time, by showing respect. This is time proven, not my theory. I will teach this along with the subject and show it in my attitude toward my students. To get respect you have to first of all give it. Mia and I just took my last class on a backpacking trip on horses to the backcountry.

We had such a great time; it was not for anything other than having fun, and we did. We will have a relationship forever with those children. I gave them all As for the semester.

Why did we do this? Mia and I wanted to cement our relationship with my class, so they would always feel close enough to come and share their lives with us.

I went to college so I could make a difference, to teach a subject but along with it, the principles of life. Because no matter how much you know, you will be hindered because of not learning the importance of respect and relationship.

I want quality people not just smart ones in my life, how about you?"

With that everyone stood up and applauded. I just reached over and hugged Mia, I was so happy for a positive response. The parents all saw that I meant what I said, and that night they saw something they all yearned for, relationship. I think we just built one with the parents.

I am sorry that sometimes we have to lose to gain, but that's what I have experienced so far in my life. My gains, however, outweighed my losses and that is always the case as children of God.

"Mr. Chairman," I said, "I would like to share what took place in class today.

"Yes, please. We want to hear what you experienced."

"I stood at the door and greeted each one of the students as they came in and introduced myself to them. After that, I said 'you are going to experience something a little different in my class.' I don't give homework, we will learn everything we need in class. I gave you name tags so I can get to know you personally, and I will grade on how you treat fellow classmates, as well as me. We are talking about respect and relationship. I told about my last class and how they will always be in our lives because of this principle. After that a student raised his hand to ask a question. Before answering his question I thanked him for showing respect to us by raising his hand, then answered his question.

As they left class I reminded them to wear their name tags tomorrow, it's going to be part of your grade. Now I am building relationship by how I conduct myself. We don't have to be buddies to gain a good relationship, that would be counterproductive, but by teaching discipline and order.

It started right away this morning when they saw who I was; children want this in their lives. Cutups, I discovered, do what they do because they are crying out for discipline and order.

I promise you we are going to make good citizens. They will be more attentive and more will stick on their minds about the subject. This is not an experiment, I witnessed this firsthand and it works. I ask you parents to hold this school accountable, you have entrusted your children to us and I take that very seriously; I promise. Let's get behind our children."

As Mia and I rode home, I said this was only the first day and wondered what tomorrow would bring.

"When you brought in Trigger into the classroom, I said to myself, this is way out, but you pulled it off. I just love you so much more each day. You keep doing things that show me I didn't make a mistake accepting you as my husband. Frank dear, you are the love of my life, next to the Lord of course."

"Well, Mia we are building relationships and if a relationship doesn't grow continually, it will die. I for one would not like that to happen; I will never take you for granted, or do anything that would cause you to disrespect me. I am having so much fun being your husband. I didn't read any books on the subject, I will write one of my own". And with that, we laughed all the way home.

I woke up early the next morning excited to face the challenges of the day. I reached over and hugged Mia and told her I loved her, we just held each other for a little while. I don't want to ever neglect loving Mia, she is worthy of more than what I can give, but don't tell her. I am so blessed, words just can't describe what I feel right now.

I hope you don't mind me mentioning the Lord as I do, because He is responsible for putting Mia and I together. He had prepared each of us, even before the foundation of the world, we are told. Just think if I had not been sensitive that day along the road when we first met, where would I be right now?

Because of being together we are both making a difference, separately it would not have the same impact on people.

I just had a thought, the Lord, Mia and I, that is three. Let's see, a uni-cycle means you (one), a Bi-cycle is (two), Tri-cycle is (three). So we are a tricycle, isn't that interesting—when people lose their balance they resort to a tricycle. All right I like that, we will now have more balance. I told Mia and Gertrude over breakfast how we have balance in our lives now with the Lord, and Mia and I.

Mom liked that and said I guess I don't have to worry about you two. Nope I said, we are covered. We three are now a tricycle and the third part is what brought in balance.

"Frank, there you go again how do you come up with these things?"

"I'm a teacher, Mia, so I have to have a sense of humor, and throw in a little imagination too.

Speaking of being a teacher, I better get on my horse, so to speak, and get ready for school. I just thought of something; since I don't give homework, I don't have to correct papers. Wow, that's awesome! I'll just have to think of ways to fill the void."

Mia said, "Frank honey, I don't think that will be a problem. You will find a way to do that I am sure.

"I have a little time so I think I will go down to the lake and spend a little time in prayer as I view the wonderful surroundings God made for us."

"I will get ready and meet you there in a few minutes," Mia said. I then rode into town again on horseback and was early, that gave me a little time with the faculty, I wanted to get to know them better. We discussed the news of the day and one of them said they heard about the PTA meeting we had last night, and wanted to know the outcome. I told them I felt good about the new relationship with all the parents and the teachers that were there.

One of the teachers said, "I heard you brought in your horse to the classroom."

"Yep, I did."

As time goes on you will see how important that was.

Last night we were showing respect with the people and my horse, very important, and I asked my horse Trigger if he would be willing to help with the event. Trigger lifted one foot and shook his head in approval. We talked about having a school event to show what Mia and I do with the horses in horse therapy.

We did this in several other schools and what came out of it was students, as well as parents, were helping people in the community with repairs and all kinds of things. And I hear it's still going on. It's about building relationship and getting out of one's self.

One person said, "I want to see how that works here, we have a lot of people on welfare that could use some help, and I am willing to do that too. I am looking forward to having your friendship and support."

There are some changes that will be going on in the children. I believe that teaching goes beyond textbooks, it's about being good examples of what kind of people we should be. I will teach it showing respect and relationship and that's how I will be building. You can report to me what you see in them if there is any change. I know that some of these children come from homes where not much love is shown, we have a chance to build character now. I'll see you at lunch, I need to get to my class before my children arrive.

Chapter 10
Making a Difference

"Good morning class, I see you all still have on your name tags. Thank you, and if you need a new one, raise your hand.

I want to go on with the subject we were on yesterday. We fought many wars since the forefathers came to America, when they were called the colonies. America is named after an Italian explorer, Amerigo Vespucci. The name America was first recorded in 1507, before that they were just called colonies. England then wanted to own the new country as they were losing a lot of their people who were fleeing the persecution they were experiencing from the Church of England.

The Pilgrims or Pilgrim Fathers were the English settlers who established the Plymouth Colony in Plymouth, Massachusetts. Their leadership came from the religious congregations of Brownists, or Separatist Puritans, who had fled religious persecution in England for the tolerance of 17th-century.

They held Puritan Calvinist religious beliefs but, unlike most other Puritans, they maintained that their congregations should separate from England's State church because of their control on them.

These people risked their lives for freedom to worship God in their own way. This did not set well with England, so a war broke out, and the pilgrims had to fight for what they believed. Most of the wars ever fought were religious wars, or about power to make everyone believe the same things. I was told that we fight on other lands to keep our land free and have liberty. Until 9/11, we did not have a war in our country after the Civil War."

"That's all for today, now let's discuss this subject and ask questions."

"Yes, Sally what is it?"

"Well, if that's why the pilgrims came here, to get away from the power of the Church of England, why are there so many different churches now?"

"Good question, and the answer is that in the original charter it was written in such a way that they would have true religious freedom. It was stated everyone should have the right to worship as they wanted, thus denominations developed. They were freethinkers, and that gives us the right to be also. But to comment on that, it doesn't make it right, God of the Bible wants all His children to be one. Jn.17: 21-It was one of the last prayers the Lord prayed before dying on the cross. Good question, Sally. (bell rings) See you all tomorrow."

In my spare time, I must get to making plans so Mia and I can have the house built before winter. So I spent some time when I got home with the ladies, they were working with the boy who was from my school. I went and saddled up Trigger and rode over to where the parents were.

I got down and asked if they had ever ridden a horse, to which the wife said she had. Would you both like to take a ride? They said that would be great, so I took them to the stables, got two horses and saddled them up. We went out in the woods and back, and ended up by the lake we developed. We got down and just had a good time getting to know one another.

Pretty soon Mia and Gertrude brought the boy over to where we were and I helped the young man down. What was that about, you ask? Again we are building a relationship between the parents and us, and Mia just included their son.

This young boy is on his way of being all he can be. Again I will say, it's all about respect and relationship which are keys to helping people through difficult times in their lives. Today, even the parents were helped with their son's problem. Our time together is already making a difference, the parents have allowed us to enter into the situation. Sometimes people won't ask for help from anyone, and that is too bad, and as a result anger and frustration set in and nothing is gained from it. There are so many people who could get beyond the physical by healing the mental.

I saw a man who was born without arms and legs surf on a surfboard, and he had a wife and children. His feet came out of his groin and hands out of his shoulders. He has made such a difference in people's lives already, and mine too. As we sat and got acquainted, I shared this with all of them.

"Mia, can I take the boy on a ride, is he all right to do that?" I asked quietly so he could not hear. She said, "yes, that would be great."

I asked the parents if they would like to go on another ride with their boy too? They agreed so off we went. The boy was on my horse with me as we are still building respect.

The boy and I talked about a lot of things, some about school and some about my past. The boy was entering into the conversation and asked questions when he found out I had a hard childhood. His parents told me afterwards that he doesn't talk like that normally but he just opened up, so now he is on the way to recovery.

Mia and her mom went into the house and made dinner and when we returned, Mia asked if the couple would like to stay for dinner since it was late. "We would love to." This gave us another chance to see how they interact together.

There is more to horse therapy than just sitting on the horse or riding it. There is the emotional part that goes along with it, getting the rock off the hose so to speak. Sometimes it takes a while depending on how deep the trauma goes. I don't know myself how far the therapy can help with the handicaps, but as time goes on I will find out. I have just started into this since Mia and I first met. The parents, at dinner, asked how Mia and I met.

I said, "Honey, would you like to tell your version?"

Mia said, she was riding her bike early one morning, got a flat tire, and had to walk her bike. Then this guy in a pickup stopped and asked if he could help me. I said that I would like a ride to my ranch if he didn't mind, to which he responded by saying, just throw your bike in the back and I would love to take you home.

"I invited him to stay for breakfast and he did, but the story doesn't stop there, he wanted to know more about the business we were in. We invited him to stay and watch as we had a client coming shortly, if he could. He did and we put him to work, and he has been working with us ever since. It's a long story how we became husband and wife, and I love this man to death. I never thought I could love a man like this, he continues to do things that make me want to hug him all the time. I have to tell you, it comes out in his working with the horses and people too.

You would not believe what Frank did at the PTA meeting the other night, he rode Trigger into the classroom."

"Why did you do that, Frank?"

"I wanted Trigger to be a part of what we were making plans to do, and Trigger was going to be part of it, so I wanted him to agree to it.."

"Well, did he?"

"Yes, by lifting up one leg and nodding his head."

Mia said the two of us are inseparable, Trigger and Frank, but I am learning about what relationship is too, and with that Mia snuggled up to me. I don't want this ever to change, and the couple saw our closeness to each other. Since their child began having problems, they told us when Gertrude took their boy in the other room, that it has affected their relationship and is the reason for wanting to see what this therapy was going to do for them.

Mia asked them to be patient and let things happen slowly and promised them that they would.

"I am so glad you are giving your son a chance to develop, he is still young enough to mold."

The couple said, "I thank God for finding you all, we already see some results, many thanks."

Mia said, "I want to warn you there will be times when he may go backward, but don't fret, it happens and we are able to get back on track again. I am so happy to have Frank in my life; he has made so many differences in children's lives too."

Mia went on to say, "I would like your permission to have your son come and spend a few hours with us without you being here. I want to have him help me brush and care for the horse we use with him, I want your son to build a relationship with the horses. This is on us, but part of his therapy too. I have seen problem children who didn't have any love in their home, looking for love in all the wrong places, turned around doing this therapy.

Your son will start doing better in school and you will see his grades go up. He soon will not be anti-social anymore, as this makes him feel more confident that he is worth something. We will work hard on this to bring him out of this dark tunnel he is in. He doesn't converse because he lives in fear, we will do our best to bring him out of that place, by giving him a new place for him to develop self-worth.

Now, none of this is on you, don't feel like it's something that you did or didn't do. It has nothing to do with any of that."

"Where did you guys come from?" they asked. "I have never met anyone so full of love and compassion."

"Well", Mia said, "sometime at your convenience we would like to share the one who is in our hearts and who you are seeing, His name is the Lord Jesus Christ. This is how He shows Himself to others, through us and people like us. So we will just continue to show Him to you until you want to hear more about Him."

"Thank you for that, we are not Christians and those who we see call themselves that, are not a good example of what they say they are. You are the first and we look forward to when we can talk about the Lord."

I said to them, "just know one thing—those who are truly Christians will have the love of Christ in them but are having issues and are handicapped too. They were forgiven when they asked Jesus Christ into their heart, they just have issues."

The family was ready to leave and said they would drop their son off after school tomorrow if that offer is still good. "Of course," Mia said, "we'll be watching for you. "

"We will never forget you." And with that, we all got hugs. That day we did more than just help a young boy, we now have a new project to bring this family into the family of God. I believe they are almost ready to receive the Lord, and the Lord is touching their hearts. We will pray for the right words to say to them now. The Lord has to prepare us too.

We keep seeing the Lord in our lives so much, even beyond the trials we experience, that we continue to give more of ourselves to Him.

We are alone now and reflecting on the events of the day. Mia said, "I love how softly the subject came into play and gave us the wonderful opportunity to bring the Lord into the conversation. Frank, I thank the Lord for bringing you into my life, I have to be careful not to put you on a pedestal. I don't want you to fall, but if you do, I hope I will be there to catch you dear."

"I would like to thank you as I am not beyond falling, and I expect the Lord to uplift me too." Mia said, "I don't want anything to change from this very moment, it is so perfect and I am falling in love all over again. Honey, I said, I find myself doing that too. I also love the Lord a lot too, after all He gave me you. He gave me a life to glorify Him with, it doesn't get much better than this.

Mia, I am so glad I don't have papers to correct so I have the time to do some things with you, and think about how I can make a difference in my students lives too. I have been given quite a responsibility."

Mia asked how it was going just doing the work in class.

"Well, tomorrow will tell as I am going to give a verbal test."

How are you going to do that individually?

"Good question, I will have to think about that."

"Could you have them all line up outside the room and call them in one at a time?"

"That's a splendid idea, Mia, have you ever seen that done before?"

"No," Mia said, "but that would work."

The next morning I wake up to Mia bringing me a cup of coffee. As I drank it we talked about the day and made a plan. Mia said we had the lad coming after school and asked if I could be here to take him on a ride.

"He really liked that, then I will have him brush Wonder, he will enjoy that too."

"Good, I will get to find out some of the things he loves to do."

I came early to class and most of the students were there already, of course I took notice and that is a consideration for their grades.

The rest of the class arrived on time and I said, "We are going to do something different today, so leave your things on your desks and follow me."

I asked them to line up single file, and said they're going to be learning one more important item for their growth today, it's called trust. I am going to call each one of you into the room one at a time, today is test day, and I will see if I can trust you to be orderly in the hall.

"Sally, you be first and it will only take a minute to do. The rest of you, I am putting you on good behavior."

"Sally, why did the pilgrims come to America before it was called that?"

Her answer was correct, so I sent her out and asked her to send the next student in. Each one had a different question, and each of them answered just right.

I called all of them in then when the last one was finished. "Class, a remarkable thing happened today, you all answered the questions correctly so you all get an A. You showed to me that you really paid attention and I thank you for your respect. I had a teacher watching you though you didn't see him, now let's hear what he has to say."

"Mr. Rogers, what did you observe when my class was out in the hall?"

He said they might have been worried about what I had in mind, but they conducted themselves very well. So, you are all learning about trust now, that goes along with respect and relationship.

"Thank you, Mr. Rogers."

"Class, I have noted that down, so you now have a credit and will be rewarded for it. When you have a certain number of credits we will do something special as a class. You get credits for a number of things, like name tags, until I think you don't need them. Talking in class you will use up credits, so let's not do that."

I can't wait to hear how the parents take this new way of teaching, when the children tell their parents what we did today. Result is my game and we are getting them, I love these children. I don't call them kids, you may have noticed that, they are deserving of more respect than that. (Bell rings).

It's a small school and this is my only class for Social Studies, so I double as a coach now. Some of the boys from my other class are in sports too. I also have an English class which I like just as much, we are going to have some authors out of this. We are going to start a school paper so they will have homework with this one, but not what I give them, rather what they find to report on.

The principal saw me out on the field and said he wanted a meeting with me after school. Oh boy, I have to go to the principal's office; I have never had to do that before—kidding!

I went to the meeting and a couple of other teachers were there along with the superintendent.

"Frank, we are interested in your method of teaching as it's so different from the norm, no homework and verbal tests! Tell us how that went please, we are not skeptics just interested. Mr. Hubert (superintendent) told us that he hired you because of all the things you did in your last school, so tell us how it went."

"Well, number one, they learned trust and respect and on the test they all got "A"s. The first thing you have to do, I find, is to get their attention. When I said no homework, I got it. They will retain the material now that it is cemented in their minds."

"Question, where did you learn this technique, in college?" "

"No, I tried this in my other class and it worked so well, and it made sense. We are living in different times now and need to find ways to get the mind to absorb information. As I was teaching, all eyes were on me, hanging on every word.".

"Why is that Frank, do you put them in a trance?"

"No, heavens no."

"Let's say you want to get hired by this person, and he/ or she is sharing with you about something they would like from you as a new employee, how attentive would you be? This is exactly what these children are looking for, they want to please and get hired. In this case, we are building relationships. I will also teach them how to find information, which as you know is what they teach in college. Children are so smart today about the internet that we can use it to teach them how to get along in this life that is before them.

I would say teach what you find comfortable, you can't do what I do and I can't do what you do. Since I started out teaching them respect, because I showed it first to them, everything else is part of the package. Teachers, it's not just about words on a page, I want it to stick in their minds.

Let me share something with you that I experienced last night. We had a seven-year-old boy at the ranch going through therapy with my wife, and when I came home I met the parents. I was told their son does not interact with people, even those his own age. Well, long story short, we took the whole family on a horseback ride and the boy sat in front with me on my horse. I let him hold the reigns and showed him how to go right or left. I was showing him that I was not going to treat him as a person with a problem, but just show kindness. I didn't treat him as having a handicap but engaged him in something he enjoyed talking about, I was not the subject he was. When we got back, he and Mia took the horses to the stables so I could talk to the parents.

They said that was the first time he had spoken so much. There is another thing, if I can take a few more minutes."

"Yes," said the principal.

"Children who don't have guidance at home or discipline come to us for that, it shows up in their behavior. They want discipline, but with kindness."

The principal had an idea, "Would you be willing to teach this to us in a class, as if we were your students in a classroom setting?"

"Only if all agree to this"—all the teachers raised their hands in approval.

"You are on to something," he said.

I said that to me the students are the building blocks of our future, so I feel the urgency to give them the tools to put that together.

"Now let me say this, you have to make the way of teaching yours, not mine, not out of a textbook or a college course, it has to be who you are. Nothing fake, something you are convinced of or the students will pick up on it, and you will be fighting an uphill battle. I want to say that I am no expert by any stretch of the imagination. I have found something that works using respect, trust, and relationship. This is imperative to begin the first moment the student walks into your classroom, they have to see you mean what you say. For example, I gave them all name tags and told them I grade differently than most teachers do. If you forget your name tags tomorrow, it will be reflected on your grade. So the first moment I was showing discipline was going to be enforced."

The principal said, "Frank, you are a genius, where did you get this way of doing things, it's remarkable."

"I take my method from my teacher, the Lord Jesus Christ. You see He works with our will, doesn't force us but teaches the three things I just mentioned, and teaches us discipline through the rewards He gives us. For example, I believe that my wife Mia was a reward from the Lord for obedience to Him.

I started out with my students by letting them know that by wearing their name tags they would get a good grade for it, so you reward discipline right off the bat. Then the Lord wants respect and shows that to us, not by putting us down, but looks for ways to show it. So He has been my teacher, and that example is giving proven results. Does that make sense? They all agreed, and I said, I must go now as I have an appointment to take that boy I told you about on a ride. We can get together again if you would like, I love sharing what I am being taught every day."

As I pulled up at the ranch the boy had just arrived, his mother took him home to eat before bringing him. I went to change clothes and get the surprise I had for him, I got him a cowboy hat as a present.

"I have something for you young man, if you are going to be around our horses you will need this," and put the hat on him. You can't imagine his reaction, he was so happy and running all around with joy.

"I am a cowboy I am a cowboy, just like Mr. Frank. I am a cowboy," and then came over to give me a hug.

"Thank you Mr. Frank, I love it."

Mia took him to get his horse and let me get dressed for riding. We rode out and started talking; I told about my day, Mia told about hers, and the boy told about his. We were interacting which he has never done before.

Why is that you ask? We were treating him as someone who had worth and value. We didn't talk down to him and he felt like one with us, still showing respect voluntarily. We made him feel like someone without a handicap. He had his own horse, too, that was obeying his commands, so he felt he was being successful at something; in this case by riding the horse. He had learned to respect the horse and every once in a while, he would rub it, talk to it, lean over and hug on the horse, and they love that.

We got back just as the parents arrived, and again their son had to take care of the horse with Mia. In the meantime, I was again talking to the parents and sharing what we experienced as we rode. They just sat there dumbfounded, it was something they hadn't expected. Mia and the boy were back and they saw him with his hat. He was so excited to show them and it was exciting to us to see how they reacted.

The dad said to us that they were wondering if we might have time to share the Lord with them tonight. Mia said we hadn't eaten yet and asked if they would like to eat with us. "We already ate."

"That's okay," Mia said, "you can sit with us and have a bite anyway, it's up to you. Then we can talk at the table if that's all right?" "Sure," they said.

"We went home last night and had a hard time sleeping, talked about it for hours, and have questions for you. We feel this is important and want someone to assist us in our lives."

Mom said there's always enough food for others so just make yourselves at home. They were taken aback as we entered into conversation and their boy joined in, and was respectful doing it. Some parents say to their children, "Children are to be seen and not heard."

"May we just go into the front room and be comfortable, and answer your questions? Mom, you too. I will help with the dishes afterwards if that's okay."

"Yes, sure Frank". So we did.

The husband began with "What is a Christian, what group is right, how do we know we are making the right decision?"

'I will be happy to answer that, these are good questions by the way. Well, we discussed this last night and just came to a blank wall." I said. "First of all, there's only one place to get true information and that is in God's Word, the Bible. What you are going to get from us is the pure Word of God, so there will not be man's version of God's plan.

Now, I would like to take each of your questions and answer it from the Word. But first, let's pray."

"Question one: What is a Christian? The word means (Christlike) and there are only three references of that word in the Bible; in Acts 11:26, Acts 26:28, and I Peter 4:16. These are man's references to believers, it is not what God calls believers. This is interesting as the Lord calls us Sons, children, heirs and brethren, but never Christians."

"Why is that? Well, Christian is a title, no family

relationship there. The Lord called the disciples brethren."

"Discussion: Why then do people refer to those who go to church as Christian? The name was given to the Apostles at the city of Antioch. But what the Lord calls those who accept Him is Sons and children of God. This is family up close."

"Question two: What group is right? That's a tough one as a lot of people don't read the Bible, they go by what that man up front in church says. If you read the Bible it tells us that to have eternal life, John1:12 tells us that as many as receive the Lord to them He gave power to become the sons of God even to those who believe on His name. You see, God wants a relationship as a family. So to answer your question, there is only one way to God and that is Christ Jesus the Lord. John 17:17 says that Christ is the Way the Truth and the Life no man comes to the Father except by Him, meaning the Lord."

"Question three: How do I know I have made the right decision?"

"We become a new creation, old things pass away, behold all things become new. Ladies, tell us what happened when you accepted the Lord into your heart."

Mom answered first: "I accepted the Lord in my early teens, I was so unhappy and frightened a lot. One day, a sister noticed I was troubled and prayed for me. I asked her if God would take away all my fears and give me joy. She said that's who He is, joy and peace. "

"I came to the Lord one night and said, Lord I am a troubled girl, I know you died for me to free me from my sins so I asked the Lord to come into my heart."

"For the first time in my life I had peace and my fears went away." There are tears in Mom's eyes as she is giving us her testimony.

She went on to say, "I think of that day now and again and it gives me such joy. Yes I saw a difference in my life, the Spirit of God came into my heart that night and I had the best sleep I've ever had."

Mia was hugging on Mom as she told her story: "It was at my Dad's memorial," Mia said, "that I asked Jesus Christ to be my Lord and Savior. The preacher said that if we wanted to see my dad again, we would have to ask the Lord into our hearts. I saw the Lord for the first time dying for me and my dad was with Him, and I wanted to be with Him too. So I asked the Lord to come into my heart. I had peace then that I will again be with my Dad." Mia was still in Mom's arms, but reached over to grab me. She went on to say that she was not a bad girl, but God says all have sinned and come short of the glory of God. "Not one sinner will enter heaven, and I sure didn't want to go to Hell for eternity."

"Do you want to hear mine now," I said?

"Yes, please, we want to hear."

So I said, "you have heard that I was in an orphanage, yes? Well, there was no love there and a lot of anger. One day the staff gave all of us Bibles, and I read in there that God loved me and died for me; no one cared for me before. I was on my way to being like so many other guys who are angry and bitter, so when I read that I wanted to know Him better. I asked Him to come into me and He did. What a change took place in me after that, the anger and bitterness was gone and life began to change for me. And now you are seeing the Lord in all three of us, that's how you know you made the right choice. The son was listening and said, "I want to know this person, you called Him Lord." Yes, I did. "How can I know Him too?"

"I want what you have, I want to be happy and kind like you Mr. Frank."

"Mom and Dad what can I say, are you ready right now too?" They looked at each other and said, "yes, we are ready too."

"Now," I said, "God's Word says that it is with the heart that man believeth unto righteousness. This means you are earnest, like you want something real bad, just like your son just told us. He wants something real bad, that's heart. Your thoughts go to, Lord I see you died for me, you love me, I want you. Can you remember," I said to the husband, "when you were about to ask for the hand of your now wife?" "Yes, I can."

"Well, that is what I mean when you want something real bad, when you ask the Lord into your heart. May we be a part of this wonderful time to see you pass from death unto life?"

"Yes, we want you to be with us as we ask the Lord into our hearts."

"Okay, each of you can pray separately and do that right now, who is first?" The son said let me be the first, this boy that had trouble talking. Mom and Dad said yes Joey, you go first. He started, "Dear God, I want to talk to you about you loving me, and want to thank you for doing that. Frank said you sent your Son to die for me," with that he broke down and then went on. "Lord, thank you for doing that. I love you, please come into my heart and make me yours amen."

The mom and Dad prayed at the same time, Dad out loud and Mom quietly but you could hear her under her breath, half crying.

"Lord Jesus come into my heart, I am a sinner that you died for. I have such love in my heart right now for you, I am so sorry for the time I used your name in vain, please forgive me. In the name of Jesus Christ, now my Lord, Amen."

We were all in a group hug, all crying. "What an experience," said the young boy, "one I will never forget." The Lord opened his heart as He did the parents. Now it's like when you got married, so I introduce you now as Children of God, and my brothers and sister in the Lord, we are family now Praise God. I am so happy.

Chapter 11
Strengthen relationships

We have made a lot of contacts and met a lot of people along the way, so it's time to show some appreciation to them, and let them know we haven't forgotten them. We have been so busy with new clients and a new school with new students. We put the house on hold for a little bit to allow us some breathing room.

Mia said she had an idea, we can invite the three principals from the two cities we held the events in, and ours here along with the two mayors, and the governor and their wives, to come to the ranch and spend the day, with a meal of course. I told her that was a great idea.

"Lets make some special invitations to send out." Mia said she would get right on it, and the dress code will be riding gear for those that want to ride, and casual for the others. I didn't tell anyone but I had a hayride in the plan too. We will have the get-together in the large arena, and will rake the dirt and roll it. We can decorate it, too, Mia said.

We got answers back and everyone is coming and excited. These are exciting times, I know there will be times that will come to test our innermost being, but we are going to savor this right now. We don't hold the future God does, and He promised not to give us anymore than we can bear so I rest on that, come what may. I said I have the day off tomorrow and thought,

"You know what Frank, this is a good time to go to visit the class of last semester and see how my former students are doing." I called ahead to the principal to see if that was all right. He said come on, that sounds like a great idea. The kids miss you a lot, you made quite an impact on them

Frank. I will inform the teacher that you are going to be here, I will tell her that it's to be a surprise.

"Thanks," I said, "that sounds like a plan. You know how much those children mean to me, they taught me a lot too. Henry, did you know what the class and I did just before school started?"

"Yes, Frank, and they won't stop talking about it. So tell me Frank, are you going to do that again?"

"You bet, we have all ready discussed making time for it; we will probably do it right through their college years."

We are slowly becoming a dude ranch, and we all Mia, Gertrude, and myself, want to do this a lot, we love people.

As you can see, this is making up for all those years as an orphan when I didn't have a family. I didn't grow up going on vacations with a mom and dad, or brothers and sisters, it was somewhat like being in prison. But now I am FREE at last, and I am glad to have love in my life and want to share it with whomever.

But, I will save most of it for Mia, she will never be left out of anything I do. Of course I asked her to go with me, even before calling Henry, and she said she wanted to go.

I said to Mia, "What do you think about taking Wonder and Trigger?"

She said, "of course, they are a part of that school too." I said, "let's make this exciting, we'll take them in the trailer until we get close, otherwise it will be a long ride. Also we can dress up in our outfits, let's make this a special treat for them, as well as to us, honey."

Well, you know from what happened before with Henry the principal, so don't be surprised with what may happen again. And sure enough, he took it as an opportunity for the school to show their appreciation for what we have done throughout the school and those involved, even the community. So what did Henry do? Well, wait and see and in the meantime, what do you think he did? It was the next morning and I loaded the horses while Mia cooked breakfast. We are looking forward to our day not knowing what we are walking into. We love to sing together, and we sang all the way to the city. I know we are going to be pleased with this day whatever happens.

I said, "Mia I think we are close enough, so we'll ride the rest of the way on horseback."

We got Wonder and Trigger unloaded and we mounted them and rode into town. Well, this is what we saw riding up to the school: all the children were with their respective teachers and as we rode up, all stood and applauded as we dismounted. We walked the horses up to where everyone was to show our appreciation—we had the horses bow along with us. Everybody was really enjoying seeing how the two of them obey us, and saw how we were really pleased with their welcome too.

Henry came over and guided us to the auditorium where they had decorated the place for us the day before, a lot of the students stayed after school to help. Another surprise, the band was there and when they saw us coming in, began playing our special song, "I Love You Truly". We went up on stage and the place was packed, some of the parents were there. Henry set all that up.

Henry, the principal, then spoke to all of us about how he too had been a student of Frank's. As I watched him help develop our children, I learned a lot.

"And now," he went on, "we have selected one of the students from each class to get up and read a piece they wrote to show their appreciation to Mia and Frank for all their efforts in teaching them to be the best they can be."

Mia and I were blown away with the love that was shown to us. As we talked it over afterwards, I said we did more than teach about trust, respect, and relationship, through it they have developed into some great people with some real special talents. But guess what Mia? It is developing us, too, we are not the same people either.

It was my turn to speak after the last student, I was almost without words though. These are very special students and outstanding individuals who will be an asset wherever they may go, and just think they are only in middle school.

"I would like to thank all of you for this special occasion, it is more than we deserve, but that's what sets you apart. I thank the staff and you students for making this event so special to us. I will never forget this time, you will always be in our thoughts and prayers no matter where life takes you or us, that you will continue to grow in showing wherever you go what relationships are all about. I can't leave you parents out of this special time, as you are a very vital part. I am seeing you through your children, let's all keep working together for everyone's good."

"Someone said once, I believe it's in the scriptures, that one who waters a garden also gets their feet wet. So as teachers, we should be getting better right along with our students. I am not the same person either; you have all helped to develop more love in me for the less fortunate, through respect you show us, and in so many other ways too. We must continue to show this example to others."

"I must remember who I am, I am that orphan boy that found the Lord, and He gets the credit for this as my teacher, and I must keep myself open always for His direction. Thank you all from the bottom of my heart, and may the Lord bless your lives as He has ours. Now I would like Mia to speak, she too is my inspiration." (Applause)

"You are looking at the happiest woman in the world to have a husband that loves me so much. I was upset the day we first met, as I had a flat tire and was walking my bicycle. But had I not had a flat, Frank would have just driven by, maybe honked the horn or waved, but never stopped. I am ever thankful for my flat tire that day. Young ladies I must say to you, that I asked the Lord for a man that loved Him as much as I do. The Lord did that and much more, He sent a man that I could trust, and my respect grew right away for the respect he showed to me that day. He is truly my gift from my heavenly Father.

I was almost thirty years old, and wondered if I would ever find a man worthy of my love. I say to you wait on the Lord, ask Him to come into your life, and then ask Him for a godly man, or you guys a godly woman. I say to you both young men and young ladies, wait and save yourselves for the real deal. When you do, you will be able to have something so special that it will take you the rest of your lives to experience true love."

"No regrets, no shame, nothing to have to hide or dismiss from your thoughts, just pure thoughts of love for that special one that was prepared for you. So don't worry about the flat tires, the right one is being prepared for you, I promise."

"I want to also show my appreciation to all who have contributed to making this a wonderful day, you are all so special to us, and we have plans in the future for all of you. Please give yourselves a big hand." And Mia sat down. (Applause)

The mayor snuck in when Mia was speaking, and the principal asked him if he had a word to say, and he did.

He began: "I am so glad that I didn't miss this celebration to show my appreciation. It's not only about this special couple, but the way you all respond to what has been taught by both Mia and Frank. I am so proud to be your mayor, this has been an eye opener to me as well. So please, if there is anything more I can do for our community please ask, my door is always going to be open to you."

"Now I just got off the phone with some of my staff, and we want to have an old-fashioned country fair, and we want Mia and Frank to be included along with Wonder and Trigger. I will announce what they will be doing, if they agree, after I talk to them. These folks have and will always be a part of this city. Does anyone have a name for the fair and parade for this year? Someone said, what about When Dreams Come True? I think that says it all, unless anyone objects."

The mayor went on; "I have one more thing in the works for our high school, they have been left out of most of this that we are experiencing here. So I will be leaning on their principal, and Henry if you would, I would like to use your expertise and of course Frank's and Mia's too; to work with me on this special project I am thinking about, I would appreciate it."

"What's important is some of you young people will be freshmen next year, and this will be a good way to break into your new journey. I would like to include your parents also."

We all applauded and it was over now, but more plans. My class got together with us and we got caught up on what has been going on since the backcountry trip. They asked how I like my new school and the students. It was so interesting as it was like we were talking to old friends, which they were, but so grown up. As we were talking, the children took turns rubbing Wonder and Trigger. We're family, I said to Mia as we reflected on the events later. We all said goodbye and Mia and I rode off into the sunset— literally, not just an expression. We loaded up Wonder and Trigger and the day was almost over, and it was a good day to be had by all.

As Mia was showering I was laying in bed thinking about what Mia said to the group about how we met with her having a flat tire, and I remembered that God answered both of our prayers and put us together. As I thought about it tears came to my eyes. I said I am so unworthy of His mercy and blessings, this orphan boy.

As Mia came out and saw me, she wondered why I was crying. I said, I am so unworthy of having you as my wife and partner. She dropped onto the bed and grabbed me up in her arms, didn't say anything just held me. She finally spoke with tears in her eyes too, and said that's how I feel. We both thought, let's thank our Lord now, so we both prayed half crying and half rejoicing. She would pray, then I would. It was like both of us were having a conversation together with the Lord. I wiped her eyes and she wiped mine, and we kissed and drifted off to sleep.

I awoke the next morning and Mia was awake already, I hugged her and thanked her for taking me in that day on the road.

"As you were telling your story of how we met that day with your bike, I remembered I was out there because I was having a really bad day. All of a sudden last night as I thought about it, my whole past came up and hit me in the face again, and I said to myself that I am unworthy of you or to be so blessed."

"You accepted me that day with no reservations and I

haven't thought of my past that much until last night. As you were on the stage yesterday, I just looked at you and said to myself that is my wife, and I was so proud of you and the things you shared, it was a moment I will always carry for the rest of my life. I am not alone anymore, you thrill my heart, and you are the flame of my candle and the love of my life."

Mia said, "I am thankful for this time we are now sharing with each other. And I thank you for the respect you show to me, the trust and honor, we have that relationship you have been teaching the children about. Thank you, dear."

I am off to school, I wonder what I will learn today; you know in life there's so much to discover. I learned in college that to be a good teacher you must be first a good student.

Mia said, "yes, I know dear and we are learning those things together, and I am also one of your students!"

"I'll let you know how the day went, as we know each day is not routine anymore."

I turned on some hymns on my way to school to help me get past the drama of last night. I need to hear from my Father, He speaks to me through some of those wonderful hymns. One I like is, (Your grace still amazes me). I was told by one of the teachers that the principle wanted to see me as soon as I came in. I hurried because I wanted to be in class as soon as the students came. Sometimes they are early, that means I have to be early too. I was going to ask him for a later time if he would, so I could greet my students when they arrived. So when I got to the office that's what I asked, and he granted my request. I wondered what he wanted though, what was so important to want to see me so early? Well, I'll have to wait for break time. I just barely got to the classroom when the first student came, and she was excited to ask me a question.

"What is it?" I said. She wanted to hear about what happened yesterday because she heard from some of the teachers about me going to see my former class.

"If you don't mind waiting until the rest of class comes,

then I won't have to repeat myself again."

She said, "all right, but did you take Wonder and Trigger?"

"Yes, we did and I can tell you, this was an afternoon I will not forget in a very long time."

I asked her too, how her parents are accepting her choice in what she wants to do for an occupation. She said I helped a lot and thanked me for doing that.

So, I said, "we have to get busy and have you work with Mia and the livestock to see if you still want to do that. Some of the cows are ready to calf now, I think it would be a good time to learn what it's all about."

"I would love that," Betty said. "Let's talk after class, then."

Now that the class is all present, I start by saying, that some wanted to know what happened yesterday when we went to just visit my former class.

Well, I called ahead to the principal and he was all right with it, so Mia went with me and so did our horses Wonder and Trigger. When we got there the whole school was outside to greet us. We were then escorted into the auditorium and as we entered, the band played our favorite song, "I Love You Truly". On the platform were some of the students from my class, and others, along with the principle.

The principal was the host and did the introductions. He first acknowledged all of us, and then he gave a short speech and turned to introduce the students who had written a speech for us. Then I was up next, but because I was so surprised, I didn't know what to say. I was sort of speechless but it worked out all right. After all, I am a teacher and should know what to say, right? I started by saying that we didn't expect all this, but it's great and thank you all so much from both of us to show us this respect and honor. I sat down and the principal introduced Mia.

She began by thanking everyone for making today a day we will never forget; and parents she said, to you we extend our love, and to you too Henry, and all you students, and a special thanks for those of you who wrote speeches. I also want to give a special thanks to you, Mayor, for taking the time out of your busy day to be here. I guess I have to ask your forgiveness, as it was because I fell in love with your teacher that he transferred to the school in my town and that's where our home is now. It was going to be one hour each way each day. Both your principal and the one from the other school gave their approval to do this, however.

Today was so you would know we haven't forgotten you; and want all of you parents and faculty and students, to always feel you can come and see us. We would love to have you any time. Frank and I feel that you are like family to us, and we don't want to lose that relationship. Then Mia gave some needed instruction to the students and sat down.

The principal again spoke and said we are all here to show to you that you are not only missed, but we will never forget you or the lessons we learned from both of you. And we all thank you for the opportunity to be able to show it to you. Our school and our town will always be indebted to you for opening our eyes to see the importance of sharing what we have with others.

He then introduced the mayor who had come in while Mia was speaking. He began by greeting everyone, us in particular, and apologized for being late. He went on to say, "we are a community of friends and neighbors now and my door is always open to any of you. This couple is remarkable and I have something for them, can we have a drum roll please." We were then presented with a large plaque that was carved and colored with Mia and I with our two horses on it. The inscription read, "To a team that made us think about others before self." I cried and so did Mia. Class, this was over the top.

I had brought the plaque to class but turned the face away until I was able to share it with them. Of course they all applauded when they saw it. About that time, our principal walked by and stopped in to see what all the noise was about. He saw the plaque and said, "That is beautiful, and so deserving." He then spoke a few words of appreciation for the privilege of having me in their school. I was not doing well with all of this, I felt so unworthy and I am, after all, just a normal human being. We had a few more minutes, so I addressed the class and told them that I wanted to teach them to be outstanding citizens that will one day be appreciated too. The secret is in trust, respect, and relationship and you are on your way to making a difference wherever you are. I dismissed them for their next class and went to meet with the principal. I didn't tell them that I broke down the night before when everything came to a head.

When I got to the office and sat down to see what the principal wanted earlier, he started with congratulating me over my so-called achievements. "I told him that I didn't feel deserving of all that and was having a hard time accepting it all, but thought about it and now my students have a mark to strive for. I will continue to press them for being all they can be and they are learning better than I expected. As you know I give verbal tests, not written ones."

"So Frank, that is what I wanted to talk to you about. Your teaching methods are so different, but are getting results. I was wondering if you might teach them to the rest of the teachers."

"Have you discussed this with them yet?"

"Yes, and they are all willing to go through some training."

"Well, I want to know where and when will this take place. I also have a few reservations. For example, I have things to do at home after work, then there is spring break when families go somewhere, so let's think about summer when we will have time, what do you think about that?"

"Let me think about it and talk it over with some of the teachers." I said that sounds like a plan, I do want to share what I have found to be a great tool. "Thanks."

I got home and Mia had just come in from her last client for the day.

I said, "Mia I am going to change my clothes and I want to go to the lake with you, I need to talk with you is that all right?"

"Yes, I'll go change too." We got to the lake and she

asked how my day turned out.

"Well, that's what I want to talk to you about." I said, "I got some help from the Lord about how I was taking all the things yesterday that caused me to break down again. I felt so bad for you to see my weakness."

"Stop right there, Frank. I want you to listen to me seriously. What I saw last night was a man who was not afraid to show his emotions, that is strength not weakness. Let me repeat that, that is strength not weakness. You also let me see your heart that you are the real deal, not putting on a front. Last night I held you until you fell asleep. I cried out to the Lord and thanked Him for a man that allowed me to see him from the inside out. He is someone I can lean on, he is real and I love him more tonight than before. Help me to use his strength to build my life on. I want this so much Lord, and thank you for thinking I am worthy of such a man."

"You grabbed me so tight and cried out and said thank you for being you, and kissed me all over, with both of us crying. When I was growing up I got such a whipping that I vowed never to allow anyone to see my feelings again; I was never allowed to show them."

As we were still holding each other, I said, "I just could not believe anyone would do that to you Mia, I am so sorry, but it is all behind both of us now." I told Mia that everything came together from all my life, too, and that praise we were getting was over the top. But today, I saw for the first time what happened at the awards ceremony through something I was teaching today.

"What happened yesterday was about trust, respect, and relationship. I told the class that I was going to be pushing them towards that. Without that award I would just be another teacher, but now I am showing that a common person can make a difference."

"So that brought me out of that deep, dark hole I was in. And now we can move forward again, with renewed energy."

"Mia, thank you for your love and patience and for the fact that you didn't put me down. I love you so much, you are God's gift to me for all I suffered."

"So how was your day?"

"I spent most of my day," she said, "praying for you. I think I ran out of tears at some point and Mom wanted to know if there was something she could do. No, I am asking the Lord for His help. I asked Him to reveal to you, Frank, that you are not weak, but strong; to know that I would always be at your side no matter what, I love you and would die for you."

I said, "Mia you are something else, not many women would agree with you in that.:

"Well, I guess we had our first trial" she said, "and thank the Lord He balanced the boat out so we didn't sink."

I went on to share what happened today, that "the teachers and principal want me to teach them the new method I use in teaching, and it looks like it may be at summer break. I told him that I was busy after school at home and didn't want anything to interfere with that, and maybe the teachers are as well." Mia said, "that will be good and won't be distracting."

Mia said, "she would like to go and share what we talked about with Mom. She was wondering if she could help me earlier when I was crying and praying for you, and I would like to tell her what has taken place to thrill her too."

We did that and Mom said that she is so elated to be allowed to see the Lord work in us.

Chapter 12

Putting everything together

To start this part of our story you have to realize that we have a lot on our plate. With Mia and her mom's business and my career as a teacher, and also the extra things we put in all that; we are somewhat overwhelmed. We are looking for someone to fill in between all that and help us out so we can fulfill our dream in helping people to excel; both the handicapped and kids.

Just a little time ago I was single and teaching students, and just taking everything in stride. But I was missing something in my life. That's when I took a ride into the country to try to sort things out, and that's when I found Mia. From that time on, life took a turn for the better. I want to share my life now with you, and show you a life that is so great. It started when I met Mia and finding out her business with horse therapy. I could see even greater potential in teaching my students about what my adopted dad taught me, to think of others more then you think about yourself.

Some children are self-centered and I wanted to distill in their minds that there are people who can't help themselves and need us to come alongside to help. That's when we brought the horses to the school, and the events that followed made quite a difference. Through that demonstration it did happen and many were out of themselves. And as you remember, even the parents got involved in helping people in the town who needed it. Having said that, things evolved and here we are overwhelmed to be able to accomplish all that. We now have the invitation we gave to the principals and their wives to spend the day with us. Also, later we have the workshop working with the teachers.

The principals weekend is upon us, and that is going to be great.

There is a caution, and that is not to take on any more activities, as we are maxed out already. The day has arrived and we are all just enjoying the relaxed feeling away from our jobs. We started out by having Mom's sweet rolls and coffee, then Mia took all of us on a tour of the ranch proper. We had horses ready for whoever wanted to go on a ride, and then we would be having lunch out at the far lake, Mia's and my favorite spot. All of them wanted to go on the ride so it made it easy to do this, and Mom would bring lunch out with the help of our staff on the wagon that we used with the children.

We were all having a great time and it was a special day. We saw deer, all kinds of birds, and even a bald eagle, which I have never seen before. We all let our hair down, so to speak, and are just enjoying our time together. I respect authority but this is different, we are just people who are having a great time, enjoying clean air and away from our responsibilities to just relax. We were joking and laughing, almost falling off our horses.

So special an event that all of us will remember for a very long time. We got to the lake and dismounted and some had bathing suits under their clothes, they came prepared for anything. I always carry my fishing pole, so you know what I was doing. Some of the guys who were with me were reminiscing over when they grew up and went fishing. I said I am sorry I didn't bring more fishing poles with us, didn't think about it, I just always carry mine with me on my saddle.

Well, here comes Mom and announced lunch by a bell, she thought of everything. Now it's perfect, she brought out tables and chairs too. Mom is a great sport and loves being a part of our lives, but she allows us time to ourselves too. She is the mother I never had, so special. So Mia and I talked it over and we are going to take Mom to Maui with us at summer break. It's neat watching her, you would never think that she is as old as she is.

We stayed out at the lake until sunset, which was not a problem as the moon was still bright to ride back with. I built a fire and we sat around it and told stories. This is only something that I read about, as I never had this opportunity as a child. Of course we brought marshmallows with us, and took turns sharing them as we roasted them. One in the group said this brings back so many memories when I was a kid and did this with my family, others chimed in too.

This was not an activity that Mia and I were just going to cross off the list. No, this was a must for those who are working with children and helping to frame their lives. They needed to step back and remember when they were children. This is going to have a great impact on their working with the teachers, and Henry was the first to tell us thank you, for bringing us back to reality and remembering about when we were young.

"This is so valuable to us as those who have been given care of people's children, even though they are required to go to school. Mia and Frank have helped us to be more than just administrators, also caring about the outcomes of children's development. I, for one, will take this through my office and see to it that all of our teachers get this."

I broke in and asked Henry if he would like to come when we have the teachers here to teach them my method for getting into the hearts and minds of our children, if so you are welcome.

One of the other principals asked what that was about.

I said, "this was to be a treat away from work, so I'd like to say you all will be included, is that all right Mia?"

"Yes, of course, the more the merrier."

"How about the rest of you, is that all right with you too?" They all raised their hands.

"Good, let's get back to fun time." Now the sun was down and all the couples including Mia and I were in a romantic mood. I was feeling a little bad, as Henry is a widower and had no one to hold, and that was the case with Mom too. So what do you suppose happened? Yes, Mom came over and sat close to Henry.

I felt so good that she did that, now they were enjoying this time too.

"It's time for us to head back, anyone who would like to stay over there is plenty of room," Mom said.

On the way back, several couples rode double and just held the extra horse next to them. Mia and I started it and some of them followed suit.

Henry asked if he might stay over as he has no one to go home to. "All my kids are on their own now."

Mom said that would be just fine. That gave us a little more time with Henry, so the next day came and we had a great breakfast made by Mia and her mom, Gertrude.

I asked Henry if he might like to go to church with us, and he said he would, "But I don't have church clothes."

Guess what, do you have any idea what is going to happen? Yep!

Mom said, "You know what, I may just have some for you in my closet." And sure enough she fixed him up, now his excuses are all gone, if he ever had any.

Do you have any idea what will come next, do you want me to go to a commercial and let you think about it? You can stop and give some thought to it if you would like, no? All right! Mia and I went out and got the buckboard ready that I had been working on for an occasion such as this. I had been repairing it and had it painted. We hooked a horse up to it and took it to the front of the house. Mia and I had Wonder and Trigger saddled up, and brought them on the back of the buckboard, and here comes the couple down the stairs.

I said "Henry, you and Gertrude have the buckboard and Mia and I will ride behind you. If you don't know how to drive it, just let the horse take you, he knows the way."

"Thank you very much, but I know how to do this," Henry said jokingly. I said, "all right, see you at church." He looked so good and they were a great looking couple together.

We arrived and as Henry was helping Mom down, Mia and I just sat on our horses and admired them, they were so cute together.

We all went in together and I was introducing Henry all around, and then my new principal came in. We all sat together and sang so loud because we were thrilled about all that has taken place over the last two days, and it is still happening. When the sermon started, I handed my Bible to Henry and looked on with Mia. Most times you don't even need a Bible as the preacher starts with one verse and then takes off from there. This is getting exciting, I wonder where this relationship is going. No matter how it does, I think the world of both of them. After the service we visited with different ones in the congregation for a while, and Henry said afterwards that he really had a good time meeting everyone.

As we were about to go, my principal asked us all out to dinner at the local restaurant, and I asked Henry if he was all right with that.

He said he was, "I can't turn down an offer like this," he said. We all thanked Larry, my principal, for dinner and said our good afternoons and headed back to the ranch. I asked Mia on the way home if I could take Henry for a short ride, I want to find out where he stands with the Lord.

"Honey, I think that is a super idea, yes do that." So, just before Henry went upstairs I asked if he would like to finish out the day by going on a short ride with me, just the two of us. He was delighted and said it would give us a chance to get to know each other better.

Henry went up to change into his other clothes, and so did we. I gave Mia a hug and was off. Both of us mounted the horses, Henry on Wonder and me on Trigger and off we went. I said to Henry, you really look good on the horse. Henry said that when he was growing up his parents had a farm and he had his own horse, so all that has happened the last two days has brought back memories. We got to the spot I wanted to get to, so we dismounted and sat in the grassy area. We talked about how Henry lost his wife and how it has affected him. I asked how he got to where he is in his profession and what he taught before that.

"Henry" I said, "I hope you are all right with all my questions, I just want to know so I will be able to help you and really be a friend."

Henry responded with, "I like that you really have a heart, Frank."

"If you don't mind," I went on, "I would like to know where you stand with the Lord".

Henry said, that when he was in college, "There was a student that kept asking me to receive the Lord into my heart. So a time came that I was having issues, and I asked the Lord to come into my heart. He has been my best friend ever since. Thanks for asking, Frank. I've wanted to tell you but never found a good time because I wanted it to be special, and this is it. I think the world of you Frank, and Mia too, I have a family I feel now, and I have been a fish out of water for a long time."

I told Henry, "we have something in common in our lives, and I am so happy too. Now we are brothers and my family is growing, I can't wait to share this with Mia, who along with me, has been praying for you."

"Now lets get down to brass tacks, I would like to know how many of your students we can count on for the fair that the mayor wants to do. Mia and I are really excited about an old-fashioned country fair." "I'll let you know, Frank."

"Henry, I am just a baby Christian, so how long have

you known the Lord?"

"Well, to be honest with you as I said I was in college, so it's been a long time. I haven't studied my Bible that much, so I am not where I should be." I asked Henry what he felt like doing about that.

He said, "what if I came once a week and we all studied together."

I said, "I don't even have to ask the ladies about that, I say yes, let's do it. But now I better get you home, tomorrow will come soon enough."

We got back and Henry went in the house to say goodnight just like a gentleman would. I said, "Henry would you like to tell the ladies what you shared with me?"

Henry said, "you mean about the Lord?"

"Yep, that's the one." Henry went on to tell the ladies that he had accepted the Lord years ago, but hasn't grown much. "Frank asked me what I wanted to do about that, and I asked if we might have a Bible study out here once a week." Both the ladies said yes, we would love it and he got hugs. Now he too has a family.

We said goodnight to Mom, and headed to take the horses to bed them down. As Mia and I were laying in bed reflecting on the day, Mia broke in and said, "Frank you don't have much trouble talking to people about the Lord, do you?"

"No, especially those I know."

"Frank, can you teach me how to do that?"

"Yes, it's real simple. You have to see that person you want to talk to in the flames of hell, and it takes all the threat of losing a friend away. You are again thinking of the other person more than yourself now. But they have to see that you really love them and are not condemning them."

Mia said, "That makes sense, thank you for sharing that with me."

"I have an advantage over you honey, because I haven't had many who I can call my friends or family for that matter, so because of that I don't have to worry about rejection. The ones who do come into my life I want them to be with me in Heaven, and it drives me crazy to think of them going to hell."

"Frank, you are still teaching me and I have such a desire to know more." I said, we "will learn together and that is going to make our Bible study even greater, and now we will have Henry growing with us. Mia, it is my prayer that I will never do anything that would tarnish your respect for me, I love you so much."

It's a Monday morning after, with no hang over, just a sense of calmness as we all are at breakfast and reflecting on the weekend. Mom said she hadn't had a time like that in a long time, and then Mia and I gave her the look.

Mia said, "you know you can't fool us, Mom."

She said, "I know what you are thinking, and it's not like that, you two matchmakers."

"Well, tell us what is like then, we are all ears."

She said, that it was a good feeling to be with a man her age. "I know Frank, you are a peach, but it's different."

"Yap," I said, "I am spoken for and Henry isn't. He is going to be spending a lot of time with us, so just enjoy your time together and forget about us, we love you, Mom." And I said, "you couldn't make a better choice."

"All right, Frank, that's enough now." We all laughed, and I kissed them both and headed off to school.

As I entered the lunch room to visit with the other teachers, one of them said, "We talked with Larry, our principal, and he said he asked you to have a workshop for all of us, and show us your method of teaching, is that right?"

"Yes, it is, but only if you want to participate, this is going to be on voluntary basis."

They all said, "they were in, and that we will be better teachers because a good teacher is first a good student, you taught us that already."

"All right, but don't think I am any expert as I am learning right along with you, my students teach me a lot. I learned a lot of what I will be sharing from Mia and Gertrude, her mom, as they work with handicap people doing horse therapy. I just use the principles I have learned from them."

I got to my classroom, and I guess I took too long with my teacher friends; so all my students were lined up in single file in the hallway.

I said, "what's up," as I stood at the door.

"We thought you were going to give a test today, so we are ready for it."

I cocked my head and squinted and just stood there with my arms folded on my chest. I broke silence and said,

"What's up, there's no test today, maybe you are giving me one, huh?"

"We just wanted to be at the door so you could greet each one of us personally is all."

I put my hand under my chin and said, "I think there is more to it than that, so what is it?"

"We just want to show you respect,"

"I am still suspicious of what is going on here, guys."

"All right, we thought if we showed you this respect that you have been teaching us, we might be invited to your ranch maybe."

She had a questioning look on her face as she said that. "That still doesn't make sense so let's just go in the room and I will sort it out later." I did greet each one as they entered the room and said, you guys are too much.

They all sat down and looked straight at me, some with elbows on their desks, others had hands on their chins. I had a captive audience so I broke in and said, "you all are very special to me and for whatever it's worth, I appreciate your respect, but you didn't have to do that to be invited to my ranch. I will be doing that when it's a good time. Now let's get to our lesson today, open your books to page ### and Jeff, please read for us. "

We finished and I was still puzzled as to what just took place, these children are really funny, but I love them to death.

I got home and the ladies wanted to know how my day went, so I told them the same story as I am telling you.

Mia chimed in and said, "honey those children love you, now you have their attention, what's next?"

"I don't know what to do, what do you gals think I

should do?"

"I think that might have been the wrong question to ask them."

"What do you think about having a mockup civil war on our property?" Mom said.

I asked how we would do that, and Mom said, that one time Mia's dad had the Army reserve come out and do that. "So we can call and see if they would do it again."

I said, "I think that's an excellent idea. Would you do that, Mom?"

"I will" she said, "I really learned a lot when they did that before, do you remember that Mia?"

"How could I ever forget it, it is one of my fondest memories of Dad, I will never forget how he always did things to help me learn to be thankful for our freedom, he was a special dad."

I said, "he sounds like a man after my own heart."

"Well, that's just one more thing to put on our agenda gals, are you all right with this idea? I personally think it's great, but maybe a little over the top."

"I have a question, how far do we want to take this if we can get the Army to do this for us."

Mia suggested to have the whole school observe this, after all it is in our history.

"I will run this by Larry the principal and see what he thinks about it, he might even be helpful with you Mom, to get this across to the Army reserve."

As you read this, can you see what this orphan boy was brought into? What if I hadn't stopped that day and helped the young lady out on the road with her flat tire, none of this would have ever happened probably.

Chapter 13
Ranch part of history

*I*t's daybreak and a glorious day too, the rooster is crowing and the air is full of new excitement ready for us to enter it. How can I ever thank the Lord over all His creation, to allow me to be part of it, why me I thought? We have another day to experience His goodness. I was on my knees to ask the Lord to help me be a blessing to someone today, then Mia slipped out of bed and came alongside of me and prayed too. We just held each other and almost knew each other's thoughts. She kissed me and got up and skipped off and beat me to the shower. So I sat there and read my Bible. "This is the day the Lord hath made, I will rejoice and be glad in it."

We got dressed and went to join Mom for breakfast; she enjoys making breakfast for us. We talked about what each of us will be doing, Mom is to call the Army Reserve to see about them putting on the show for us. I went to school and asked the principal for a time I could talk to him. He said, perhaps after your class is over. This time I was able to get to my class before the children. In the meantime, Mom called the Colonel at the Army base and told him that we wanted to have the whole school witness the battle of the Civil War like they did once before at our ranch.

He said, "I remember that, the funny thing is, we were just talking about doing that and didn't know where we could do it. Yes, we will be happy to help with that."

Mom asked for a day that we could have a meeting with him and his staff, so he told her when. Now I have to talk to my principal Larry to get his permission to take the school out to the ranch. My class ended, so I went to Larry's office and he said, "come in Frank and have a seat. What are you up to now, Frank?" Something special, I hope.

"Yes, Larry, as you know I have been teaching on world wars, and showing how most of them are religious wars, but now I want to show them about the war that was between the states, the Civil War. Mia's mom mentioned that the Army Reserve put on a mockup war at her ranch when Mia was just a little girl, so she called the Colonel on the base and I just got word from Gertrude that they are willing to do it again. They said they still had the equipment but some of it is in need of repair."

Principal Larry said, "he wanted us to help with that." "So, I need your permission to take all the children out to the ranch."

"Yes, of course, let me know when you want to do this. Would you prefer doing it on a Saturday, maybe?"

"I will run that by the others,"

I said, "and see, but would you be willing to have it during school time?"

"Yes, but I would rather do it on a Saturday."

"Frank, I want to share something with you about what I learned concerning your ranch. I went online this morning after being with you last weekend, and I truly want to thank you for my wife and I, we had such a lovely time. But, guess what I found out? The Civil War was partly fought on your ranch property, can you imagine that?"

"No way, really? Wait until I share that with the ladies, it will blow them away. You are sure, Larry?"

"Yes, and I will give you the website so you can see what I saw. I feel now that we can't keep this to ourselves, it belongs to the town."

"We will have a meeting to get everyone on the same page. What's a good time for you Larry, what about this Saturday? That will give me time to call the mayor, too, and include him into our plan."

I got home and told the ladies about what Larry discovered online about our ranch being in the Civil War. That means there would be artifacts on the property. Gertrude said her husband suspected it but never investigated.

"I don't know if this is a good thing, we will have people trespassing on the property to find relics."

"Well, as long as they behave themselves I don't see a problem with that, do you Mia?"

We had our meeting and it was decided to do it the following Saturday. In the meantime, we gave the Army permission to come and practice on our property. We mulled it over and thought about a write-up in the local paper advertising the event. We will have to be willing for anyone who wants to see the mockup to come too; it will be standing room only. I told my class about the plan and that they are going to get to come to the ranch, but I will have them write a paper on the event. And the best one will… well, you'll find out. Until then, we will study the subject to be well-versed on what we are going to see.

I called Henry and told him what we planned, and that he was invited, but not to breathe a word of it in his school. We will have a time to do it again for them too, but much later. He was thrilled to be included, and asked if he could come the night before and stay with us at the ranch house.

I told him we would be delighted, "Can you be here for dinner Friday night, Henry?"

"Yes, Henry" said, "I could be there around 6 o'clock if that is all right?"

I told him that was fine.

When I shared this with my ladies Mom was all aflutter, and all smiles too. I asked if we could dress up in country clothes and really make this more like an old country ranch?

They looked at each other and Mom spoke and said, "yes, we could. I will have to make one of those fluffy hats for Mia. I have mine, feeling like a country boy, Frank, where did you come from? You're so much like my late husband it isn't funny."

I said with a grin on my face, "we will make Henry feel right at home and he can change into Pa's clothes like he did before."

"So tell me Mom, what needs repairs? You said the Colonel mentioned some of the things need fixing." "Well, Frank most of it are the clothes, so Mia and I are going to do some of it in the next day or so."

The days just clicked by and we were all ready for the event, Henry came as he said he would and was all excited come Saturday morning, just like a little kid. We went out to feed the horses and Henry fits in great. Not like my image of a principal, just a great friend. "Frank," he would say, "you are bringing back so many memories of my past, and I love it."

When we got back to the ranch house, cars were arriving and my class was doing what I told them, and that was to meet at the front of the house. Henry and I already had the wagon ready and as my class came I had them get in. There were seats on both sides for them to sit comfortably. They all had their notebooks; remember they are to tell a story as a contest, so they are eager to do well and take good notes. This is another way to set things in the mind, they will never forget the lesson in their whole lives. When they have children, I imagine they will be telling them about what they learned in school and at our ranch about this.

In anticipation of a lot of people coming, with cars and buggies, also on horse back, the ranch hands were around to keep all of that orderly; cars in one place, wagons in another, and of course a place for the horses to be tied up. Now we are all together, and waiting silently to be shown history in the making. My children were all smiles, pencils and notebooks in hand. Their parents stood beside our wagon and Mia, Mom, Henry and I were in the seats up front facing the field.

All of a sudden, out of nowhere, the confederate army came dashing up with a cloud of dust behind them into the field and the regulars were already in the field hiding; they came early and we didn't even see them. Shots were being fired, men falling off the horses onto the ground. People with some sort of red badge ran out and drug them to the side and were hovering over them. Suddenly a cannon went off and scared the life out of us. There was smoke all over the place, and of course the regular army won the battle.

It went on for about an hour and a half, quite a show,

and really brought to light how devastating war is.

All the troops and people came to the place we had set up for refreshments and a place to get acquainted with each other. Some had not seen each other for a very long time, we had anticipated this and just let people spend as much time as they wanted. Old relationships were being re-established and many of the townspeople showed up too, making this a fantastic time to get reacquainted, and also form new relationships. I don't know where this will go, but it is definitely a success, even more than anticipated.

The mayor took us aside and congratulated us for doing this, and wanted to get to know us a little better.

Mom said, "Mayor, you are welcome to come out any time and get to know who we are and what we do."

He thanked us for that and ended by saying, "We'll be in touch." I said, "when he couldn't hear me, to the ladies, I don't know what that meant, but I suspect something is in the air."

I got all the children together without their parents, but with Mia and Mom, and introduced each one to them. I said, "we did this for you but others wanted to be included, so we will have you out soon, just you, and we will spend a couple of days together. Would you like that?"

They were all excited and with all their voices let us know how excited they were. So with that, I called the parents over, introduced Mia and Mom to them, and let them get acquainted with each other.

One of the ladies said she loved our outfits, Mom said, "These are not our outfits, this is how we dress normally."

Henry was in earshot and was snickering as he too was dressed in old-fashioned clothes. Henry was then invited to stay over and spent the weekend with us. He said, "I was hoping you would say that. I came prepared, and to go to church too."

Gertrude and Henry are really enjoying each other, I wouldn't be surprised if someday Henry would pop the question, we will see. Henry said he brought his work clothes with him, so if there is something he can do let him know. I told him there is always something to do on a ranch like this.

"I am about to go out and spend a little time brushing the horses, you may like doing that too, Henry."

"I would," he said. So out we went and I let Henry brush the horses and I started cleaning the stalls. The ranch hands were all busy doing other things, so when we finished,

I said "now I will take hay out to the cattle using the wagon instead of my truck like I usually do." Henry was on the back and kicked off the bails of hay as I drove the wagon, he was really enjoying himself.

We got all our work done and it was dinnertime, and we had chicken dumplings again. I love chicken dumplings, we could smell them even before entering the house. Henry and I were off to get ready for dinner. He has becoming like the older brother I never had, and I couldn't ask for anyone better. As we sat at the table, I asked Henry to give thanks.

Wow, did he ever give thanks! He gave thanks for the birds that day, and all the events, then for each of us separately, but mainly for his salvation in Christ. We all had a loud AMEN, we have become really close to each other.

It's Sunday and we did like we did before, it is becoming routine now. When we got to church, not the building as the church are the people, the preacher asked Henry to share his testimony. Henry consented, so after all the singing, the preacher introduced Henry to the group as a person that was going to share with us today.

Henry started out by saying, "he came to know the Lord as his Savior when he was in college. There was a fellow student that kept telling me to ask Jesus Christ into my heart. I did that one day when I was in need of someone's love in my heart. My course was real hard for this country boy and you know what, the Lord helped me. Since I accepted the Lord, He has always been at my side, especially when I lost my dear wife to cancer a few years ago.

Frank, Mia and Gertrude, and I have been talking about having a home Bible study as I am not very well-versed, and I am looking forward to doing that. This is an incredible family the Lord just dropped into my life. I am so glad to have met all of you, too." and with that, Henry sat down.

The preacher got up and said, "he was equally blessed with having us in his life. Frank, would you like to say something?"

"Yes, I would."

I got up and said, "I was grateful to have met Henry, and of course all my family, but I owe so much of who I have become to Jesus Christ, who showed up in my life when I was in an orphanage. He told me that He loved me and gave His life for me. No one ever would have done this for me, instead I got beat up and switched for no reason. I will serve the Lord for the rest of my life; The Lord did something so wonderful. He also introduced Mia to me and now she is in my life as my wife, He then gave me a Mom too. How could you not love Him and want to serve Him?

You know He does all the work. It's like all He really wants is a relationship, He wants our companionship with Him. I also am so glad to meet all of you, and if there is anything we can do for you, just ask, and I sat down. "

The preacher finished by thanking us for what we contribute to this community. He went on to say how he learned a lot from the mockup at the family ranch. We left and went home, taking Henry with us of course; we then all changed clothes and had dinner and said goodnight to Henry. We just all sat and relaxed, it's been quite a weekend. But with any ranch with livestock we weren't finished yet.

"Oh well" I said, "do you gals want to go on a ride?"

Mom said, "you two go on, I think I will stay here and relax for a while."

We laughed and hugged her. As we were getting on our horses,

Mia said, "Frank, you know I don't have to use makeup as long as I am with you, because you make me blush a lot."

I had taken my guitar and put it on my saddle, and as we rode I was singing to Mia. It was John Denver's song "Annie", it's a love song. I love singing and do it at the drop of a hat, whatever that means.

One of the verses says this: You fill up my senses, come

fill me again. I will love you forever and that is no sin, come close to my heart so I can feel the beating of your heart, let me fall for you again and again, over and over I go, so hold me close and we can fall together.

"Honey I know that song, and love how you changed the words a little."

"Do you mind?"

"No, I love it. I love you and how you keep showing it to me."

I said, "honey, without smothering you, I love knowing you'll always be there; you are the energy that motivates me. I cannot imagine my life with out you in it. We compliment each other and we are truly one. So it's not about what you can give me, but what I bring to you to make us whole."

"You know, what's so important right now is to build a strong bond that nothing can break. When children come into our lives they will just enhance our love for each other, no matter what. They are not going to diminish our love for each other."

Mia said, "I love what you just said and will pray for that day that my love for you will not be divided between them and you, me too. Since both of us are looking to the Lord, we will tell them that they have entered into that relationship with us, with the Lord."

"Frank honey, we need to discuss about when to have them don't you think?"

"Yes we do, but first we have some building to do, strengthening our relationship and getting the house built. We could get along with having one child where we live now, but once it starts there may be more, and then it won't work, you agree?"

"I think we are still young enough," Mia said, "and I do agree just wanted to hear you say it."

"All right, I will start on the plans for our house tomorrow. I really feel good we had this discussion, honey."

Chapter 14
Plans for a house and events

The next morning came and I spent my extra time at school looking up floor plans on the Internet. I found one that was very close to what we talked about, it was a five bedroom four bath plan. So I printed it out and took it home that afternoon to show Mia, and both of us approved it.

The next step is getting a permit, and also to decide where we want to build it. We did say before that we wanted it by the lake we recently built. I got both permits, one for the house and the other for the sewer system. We now have to find a contractor.

Due to our involvement in the community one came to us, his name is Jack. He said he heard that we wanted to build a house and wanted to build it for us at no cost, we only need to pay for materials. Jack said that we do so much for the community he wanted to show his appreciation to us. I thanked him for his generosity, and said we would talk it over and let him know.

When he left I said to Mia, "I can't believe this is happening, but is he who we want to do this project, what do we know about him, do you know him, Mom?"

"Frank, he is a great builder, I can't believe he wants to do this, it's wonderful." Mom went on to say that she has known him as a good builder for a very long time.

I called him and, first of all, thanked him for his generous offer, and said that we had decided to have him do it. So when can you start? I asked.

I still have to get blueprints made. Jack said to bring him what I have and he will get them done for us. "I will use my architect and print a blueprint. In the meantime, I will get a lumber list together." I told Jack that we haven't done that much in our community.

"Well," Jack said, "I know you will be doing that, and this will give you the time to make your plans. Besides, Frank, you have already made such a difference in my children. You are teaching all of us through our children to have respect and trust to build relationships."

"My wife and I were having problems that I won't go into, but it had to do with not trusting or respecting each other. Our kids have saved our marriage by showing us through your teaching them. I am ever indebted to you, and my wife and I discussed what we could do for you and Mia. When I was at the city inspector's office I was told that you were going to build a house."

"All right, this will help to ease up what's in the works already, thank you from the bottom of our hearts." I got home and told Mia what took place, she got down on her knees and so did I and gave the Lord thanks. I thanked Him for all the ways He has guided us to bring us to this point. "And Lord I am indebted to you to serve you for the rest of my life for your gift to me, and for giving me Mia to always be at my side. Amen."

Mia said, "Lord I thank you for giving me a man who I can give myself to and be with him to build a relationship, and share you with whoever you put into my life, just like Frank does. Lord I love you so much, help me to always honor you. Amen"

I grabbed Mia and held her so tight, and said, "I am so unworthy to have you as my wife; and to think of how the Lord brought us together. I can't imagine how this could have happened, except the Lord knew both of our hearts. I think of all the possibilities I could have had when I was in college, but it would no doubt have ended in a disaster. I would love to look over God's shoulder to see what our future will be, but maybe that's not a good idea, He has to prepare us as we go along to handle what might be ahead. So I will take one day at a time, and ask for the strength to deal with all that comes our way."

Mia wasn't going to let me go, she just kept hugging

me. I told her that I don't want this moment to ever go away, I could stay in your arms for the rest of my life. She said, "I guess we better get on with the day though." "As much as I am enjoying this moment, you're right."

We got changed into our work clothes and went to take care of our horses, Mia got her horse and I got mine to give them a workout. We have been neglecting them a little bit and you know it's about relationship even with our horses, so we worked them really hard and they loved it. We brought them back and rubbed them down, and then put a blanket on them for the night.

I laughed and said, "Mia, we take care of our horses better than we take care of ourselves." "So" I said, "I am going to give you a rubdown."

She said playfully, "you'll have to catch me first."

I said "no problem."

So we were running around the yard like two little kids, I finally caught her.

We were giggling and just being playful when she said, "if you are serious I have some good smelling ointment I have been saving for a time like this. I have to tell you there is nothing like a good rubdown after a stressful day like we just had."

I said, "if we can do it for the horses, we should be able to do it for each other."

The next morning we had a call from the mayor of my first town, he wanted to talk about the upcoming fair. It was a month and a half away and time to start making plans. We talked about some ideas when I saw him at what turned out to be an award ceremony for us instead of us visiting my class of last year.

So we set a time to get together with the volunteers. I then went to the school and am always thrilled to be with my class, and they will be ready to help even before summer break.

I got back to my class the next morning, and Sally, who is always the first to ask questions, said, "are we going to have a test today over what we saw with the Civil War mockup?"

"Sally, that is a good question, but before I tell you, let's discuss it first. I assume you all have your papers on it, don't you? You know I am more interested in what and how you learn, not the grade. You could get an A and not have a clue about the subject."

"Sally, since you asked, let's start with you and just go up the line. Each of you read what you have written."

I was blown away about what she had learned, she even gave a summary of how it affected her and changed what she was told about it. Each one saw something different, but all contributed to fill in what others missed.

I said, "I am so proud of you all; each of you had a different view that contributed to all of us. Do you know how many adults don't know what it was about? So, I want a volunteer to share what your parent's discussion was with you after you all got home. First, how many parents had a discussion about what they saw when you got home, raise your hands?" All with one exception, and it was because his parents couldn't come.

Ken had his hand up, and I said, "yes, Ken."

He said he wanted to tell what his parents got from it. I said go ahead. "Well, we had a long talk about it and I wrote down what they told me, my dad especially."

This is from Ken's notes:

"The war wasn't only about slavery, but more about the southern states wanting to be separated from the northern states because they were always telling them what to do. My dad said that out of this was born the Republican Party under Abraham Lincoln in 1860. My dad is a history buff, and he went on saying that without the votes of the South Lincoln was elected."

"Ken, you tell your dad he gets an A for that, and by the way you all get an A today."

"Now off to your next class, but as you leave I want to say how proud I am to have you as my class, you are all going to be historians. I am going to keep your papers and make a library document of them all for this year's class; you deserve that recognition for your efforts."

This is going to influence other classes and as I teach

this method in the workshop, this idea will spread.

All systems are on go for our house. Trucks are coming to deliver materials of all kinds, and the builder and his concrete contractor are here to get started putting in forms for the foundation. I have a copy of the blueprints, so here we go. We had already determined the spot and where the front of the house would be facing. Mom came to us and said she wanted to help by paying for the material that just arrived.

"Are you sure Mom?" I said.

"Yes, this is going to be my contribution, would have been Dad's wishes too."

"All right, I'll let you and Mia take care of that. I have a meeting with the mayor to talk about the fair we are putting together, so Mia, what is a good time for you to go? I only have one client today." She said, "good, I'll come and pick you up."

We got together with the mayor and he had some volunteers to work with us. We made a list beforehand of what we proposed to do for all the decorations, and location for the equipment that we will be renting—like a Ferris wheel and other fun things that no country fair should be without.

The person assigned to work with us was Shirley, and she and Mia will do all the designing of the main street along with the stores. A lot of flowers will need to be ordered, banners, and all that goes with that.

One man came and said he had a train to donate for this event. It was used before for such an occasion and he would start bringing all the parts right away, it was one that people could ride on.

Shirley said she has a lot of people to work with us, so here we go! All parties were excited and the mayor wanted to know if we planned a parade. All of us said together, of course. So we will get posters and notify the press for people to register for the parade, and encourage people with classic cars to get them ready.

We left and I said it looks like this is going to be a fun time, and we would be able to make plans with Shirley and her team by phone. Our job is going to entail getting some of the physical things ordered for the time we need them.

It's a good thing we are still young to handle all that has come upon us. We both are thrilled to do this and strengthen our relationship with the families.

I called Henry and gave him Shirley's phone number so whatever he could offer, they could work together. I got a hold of an electrical contractor to do some lighting, and he said he wanted to install decorative lights on the main street leading up to the entrance of the fairgrounds. I said we didn't have time to tear up the street to do that, but he assured me that these lights would be wireless and controlled by computer.

"Wow," I said, "that would be great. Write up an offer and I will submit it to the committee and then you can send the contract to me."

He said it would not be necessary as he was going to do it for the town, at his expense.

"All right. Do send me a picture of them for approval." He said he would.

"I understand you are building a house on your ranch." "Yes, I am." "May I be your electrical contractor?" "Let me find out" I said, "who, if any, my general contractor has. I will get back to you on that." He answered that he wanted to 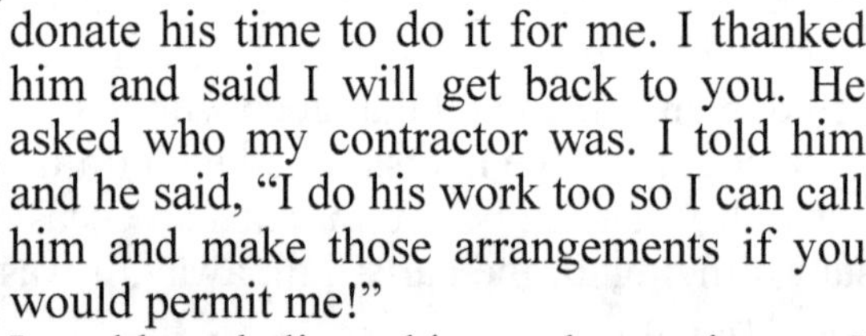 donate his time to do it for me. I thanked him and said I will get back to you. He asked who my contractor was. I told him and he said, "I do his work too so I can call him and make those arrangements if you would permit me!"

I could not believe this was happening, so I said, "go ahead and thanks so much. I really, or I should say we, do so appreciate it."

He went on to say "that he and the town were indebted to us for what we did to bring them together, you will never know the impact you and your wife had on us. So thank you Frank, for allowing me to do this for you two. "

Now, I am overwhelmed with all the generosity of people, but it is just more proof of what I teach; trust, respect, and that equals relationship.

I got a picture of the fixture and sent it on for approval, and the mayor and committee approved it.

The mayor told me afterwards that he had been thinking about doing this for a long time, they are beautiful. "I am so glad to have come to know you and Mia and still think about our time together at the lake, I will never forget it. My wife and I talk about it all the time. It was the first time we have done something like that in so long, thanks again for thinking of us."

I contacted a car club to see if they were going to be in the parade, and they said they were.

The next thing to do is contact horse clubs with Clydesdale horses. I found one and they, too, are going to be there. And I wonder who is going to be the Queen of the parade or the Marshal? We know the mayor will be in the beginning car.

Now all we have to do is start putting up the decorations, so Mia called Shirley to see how things were going.

"We're starting tomorrow," Shirley said, Mia said she would be there to help.

"I haven't been to a fair or seen a parade in all my life. Oh, I guess I better get a hold of the people with the Ferris wheel. I'm like a little kid, I am so excited to be a part of all this. Having never been at a fair, this is a stretch for me. I have to say that I have never seen such cooperation before, this truly is bringing the town together."

When we got to the town, there were a lot of people already there. Shirley was so glad to see us she was becoming a little overwhelmed, so Mia jumped right in to direct people to do this and that. It's what she is good at, and does it with a fair amount of calmness so others are more relaxed and the work goes on very smoothly. If I have an idea I go to Mia and pass it by her first, I don't get in the way.

Having said that, she puts me to work no standing around with her. I just like standing back and watching her operate. Every once in a while, I think back to where I was a year ago and before I met Mia.

We are already with three days to spare, all the lights are up and so beautiful, I thought we should have a pre-parade night, so it was announced over the local radio and this would give us a way to make sure everything went well. The mayor had a band come from the high school and middle school. They played a number of songs and the mayor went to the microphone and welcomed all of us, and of course he gave a thank you to Mia, Shirley, and me.

The day has come for the parade and the town is loaded with people from all over. The local police were very visible and also had a group in the parade. My class was in the parade dressed in civil war clothes; the parents got together and Ken's dad was at the head of it. I got really emotional—they looked so good as they marched with their band, all of which I didn't know about. I then spent time with them afterwards.

I said, "you all get an A for the semester. I thought, what's next, with all the things that have been happening over the last month."

The mayor invited the people, after the parade, to go to the park where the festival was. In these troubled times, this was good medicine for sure.

Mia and I hosted the festival and were also the Grand Marshals for the parade, so we were dressed in our country clothes. We also rode the Ferris wheel and a lot of other rides in which the mayor and his wife joined us. I know what you are thinking, where is Gertrude? You guessed it, with Henry having a ball. I think we will see them getting more serious, I am fine with it and so is Mia.

Chapter 15
Special events and awards given out

After the parade and festival Henry brought Mom home and stayed over so he could go to church with us, or with Mom maybe. We all went on a ride after lunch on our horses, and Henry is becoming like family. Henry stayed over Sunday and went to work early Monday morning, and we went to work too.

When I got to school the entire school applauded as I entered. When they were finished, I said, "now give yourselves a hand too, for all your involvement. I am so proud to be in your school, and there are a lot of events that you will be a part of. School should be not only a place to learn important subjects, but also to have fun. I want you to wake up in the morning excited to come to school like I do. Thank you all for your recognition this morning."

As my class entered the room I applauded them, especially for what they did on Saturday at the parade.

I said, "I want to know how this happened, I know your father Ken was behind it, right?"

"Yes, he was and was able to get uniforms for all of us, and for the ladies too."

"Yep, I am so proud of all of you, but let's think of something we can do for Ken's dad, any suggestions? What do you think, Ken?"

"I think a plaque with all our names on it; the heading should say something like this. In appreciation for service rendered."

"What do the rest of you think of that? Raise your hands if you agree." All agreed. "So another job, do I have any volunteers to have it made?"

Dear Sally was the first one to raise her hand. She said,

"my dad knows someone who does that." "Okay, you're hired. I want a picture of you guys all dressed up on it. Sally, do let us know how much it will cost, please, when you find out. "

"This is a class project so we will take a collection for it, and we will take this class time to each draw a design for the plaque and what it should look like. Then the one we all feel is the best will be the one we use. I will do that too, so let's get started. Be sure to put all the names on it, and I will get a picture of you all in the uniforms that you wore for the parade to put in the background."

"I am excited to do this for Ken's father. So if there is a tie, we will make one for the school, how's that sound?"

"Yes!!"

"When we get this done I will schedule a special awards ceremony."

I didn't tell my class what I had planned, I wanted it to be a surprise.

We are ready to see what the class comes up with, so I put all of them up on a board and we all voted..

"The one with most votes get accepted. I have to say they are all great but there was a tie, so which one would go to the school and which one will go to Ken's father?"

We all voted on that, and it's time to get them made.

We will have Ken's dad's picture up in the corner and all the names and year on it, class of -----. Ken's father is a local dentist, so I found myself in his office to meet him one day. Not telling him what we had planned, just to thank him for what he contributed to the parade we had.

When we met, he said, "I too want to thank you, from what I have observed so far you are quite a contribution to our community, and it's I who should be thanking you, Frank. So Frank, what makes you do what you do?"

" Well, I guess I could ask you the same question. But, my reason is so I am not just helping these children get good grades, but to know the subject when they are through."

"You probably have heard this before, but I wished I had a teacher like you when I went to school. (Ken's father's name is Bruce.)"

"Well, I went to school too, and I became a teacher to make a difference. I didn't like the ones I had, they gave homework and didn't really do the job they were hired for."

"You have made quite a difference in my son, Ken, and he is excited about going to school now, where he hated it before."

"The principal wants me to have a workshop to teach my methods to the teaching staff here in our school, and I wouldn't be surprised if the teachers from my former school would come too. We are going to have it out on the ranch in one of the large rooms in the main house, and will do it the first Saturday after school's out. Mia is going to share in the class too as she has been using some of what I will be teaching with her horse therapy business and with people, it has proven to be very successful. I will start by teaching trust and respect, which builds relationship. I have a relationship with my students, not just as a teacher, but what comes through is I care, and think of my students as having value. Well, off of my soapbox now."

"Bruce, I just wanted to meet you, and ask if we might be able to count on you for some events we have in the works; like parades and other events."

Bruce said he would be delighted to participate. Bruce also said that he and his wife talked about having Mia and I for dinner one of these nights.

"So what night would work out for you, Frank?"

"I will get back to you tomorrow on that, I am not sure what Mia is planning."

"Bruce, it's been a pleasure meeting you and I look forward to working with you. I want to say this before I leave, most communities don't realize that children are the most precious people we have, most feel they are just someone to kick around instead of being very valuable. They soon will be taking their place in society and it's at this time we have the chance to steer them in the right direction. They should never be looked at as a liability but rather an asset. "

"I know this from being an orphan who was just thought about as a throw-away kid. It wasn't until I was adopted by a man who taught me that I had value and showed me love for the first time, I felt like I wasn't a mistake like I was led to believe. So Bruce, I went through the school of hard knocks."

"Frank, you should be a professor in college," to which I said no. "So if I may, I would like to share one more thing with you, Bruce!"

"Yes, of course, we are getting to know each other and you are becoming more than just Ken's teacher, so tell me."

"I want to teach the children values now as it's all over when they get to college. If they haven't built a strong sense of respect for themselves, college will be just a playground to them. They will use it to get into drugs and all the problems that are out there, because you can't see them. It's even encouraged for the students to experience sex, just be careful and use protection they say. No, it's not all right to just be careful. They are breaking down self-respect, and I for one will never allow anyone to take that from me, it is my identity. When I have lost respect for myself, I have lost it for everyone else too. I am sorry Bruce, I have taken a lot of your time, I'll let you go back to work."

"Frank, in just a few minutes you have taught me so much, I thank you and promise to give this some serious thought. What you have shared with me not only has changed the way I will look at children, but you have helped me see what I need to change too."

Well, they have started to build our house and the foundation is going in. I asked not to have a concrete floor but a wood floor, so that means forms have to be set. So now we are seeing more progress in our lives.

I asked Mia when I got home about a good time to have dinner with Bruce and his family. I will be getting his daughter next semester, so this is a good time to get to know her too. We set the dinner for Friday night if that works for them too.

I asked Bruce the next day and he said that is a great time. I said, "I am looking forward to this time together, we'll be showing your children what a relationship looks like."

Sally brought the rough draft for the plaque to school for approval. So we all gave our approval, and it will be made soon. "Sally, when will they have it done?" She said they promised in a week, no longer.

I called Henry and our governor to ask if they want to be a part of it. This is to be a surprise to Bruce.

We went to Bruce's house to have dinner and, of course, Henry came in to be with us. He called ahead and Mom said the kids are going out for dinner, so you and I will have a nice dinner to ourselves. I'll make your favorite dinner, chicken and dumplings. Mia and I talked about a lot of topics with Bruce and family, nothing about school so the children would be more comfortable too.

The day came to have the celebration for Ken's dad. No one knew why, but my class did and it was agreed that Ken would be the one to give the plaque for doing the parade display and getting all the uniforms for the children. We just announced in the paper that we were going to recognize all the young people for participating in the parade. Our principal got up and thanked me and Mia for making all this possible. Apparently the Army heard about the awards ceremony because they showed up with their band.

The principal welcomed them and asked if the colonel would like to say a word, and of course he did. He spoke of the wonderful community and all the schools that were present to make the mockup war such a success.

He went on to say, "We of the Army Corp have a bronze embossed plaque to present. Would Gertrude, Mia, and Frank come up to the platform?"

Well, we did and to our surprise, the colonel said we want to award you for allowing us to be able to use your ranch, and we will install it in the place you want it. The words on the plaque said, "We the Army of the United States of America Battalion fifteen award this plaque to the Milady Ranch to commemorate the actual war fought on these premises as part of our history."

It also had the three of us on our horses. The band played the "Star-Spangled Banner" and all were at attention; some held their hand over their heart and others saluted, and for the first time, I saw respect for our country from all who were there.

We told the colonel thank you, we are so honored to receive this plaque on their behalf. Next, the principal asked the governor if he would like to speak next, and he did.

He then called the principals from the three schools to come up. "I have a plaque to give each of your schools for participating in the mock up war and the parade." All of the principals said on behalf of their schools, we will receive this plaque with honor, and all said thank you.

Our principal asked if there is anyone else who wants to say something before Frank takes the mic. "All right Frank, take it away."

"Greetings everyone, and thanks for being here to witness the great respect shown today, but we are not through yet. Would Bruce please come up, and all the students that marched in the parade with him."

Ken then stepped up to present the plaque to his father on behalf of his class. "On behalf of my class we want to award this plaque to you, DAD, for your generosity and putting the civil war team together for the parade. Thank you from the bottom of our hearts, and please accept this plaque from my class as our appreciation to you."

Of course you know it was a very emotional moment for Bruce to accept the plaque to start with, and then to have it presented to him by his son. He broke down to see his son and his class show such respect for him.

It's Saturday morning, and Henry did stay over, so we were all together for breakfast. Henry and I went out and fed the livestock, I enjoy his help and he enjoys it too. It brought back so many memories when he grew up on his parent's farm. Henry is becoming a very good friend to me. The ladies are cleaning up in the house. We are all finished so the four of us are mounting up for a day out in the forest. Gertrude and Mia made a lunch to go with us. So we rode out to the far lake for a day of relaxation, and just to enjoy good conversation away from work.

We got to the lake and went swimming, we went prepared and dried off to have lunch. I said "Henry, would you and Mom help with taking the children, my class, on a four-day backpacking trip?"

"Mom, we can have one of the hired hands go with us too, and bring us food. Does this sound like something that would fit into your plans?"

Henry and Gertrude looked at each other and both said, "why not, sure. I think this is going to work out great, as these children will be needing counsel and also see that grown ups can have fun too."

So that time has come and all the children were there, excited to be with us. Now this would be a nightmare if the class and I had not built a relationship first. I am not going to be a friend to them, that will come later in life. I need them to continue to learn respect for people older than they are. So far they are doing great and even their parents are telling us that, so it's working.

Well, do you remember Betty? She is with us and has been working with Mia with the horses; she's a good rider and will be a great help. We headed out and Mia is introducing some trail songs and some camp songs, the children will take these with them forever as well as the experience of being out in the woods.

One of the privileges is Henry, as the children can see that a man in his position is able to step down and just be one of us, with such insight as well. Some of the children came to Henry when we were at the campsite, asking him questions to help them.

We had fun watching the interaction between all the children and everyone. We had the chuck wagon and one of the ranch hands with us; he was a good cook too and had fun with the children. Having respect for each other doesn't mean that you can't have fun. We are on the way back home now as I have that meeting with the teachers on Saturday.

Well, here we are. Of course Henry stayed and sat in with us, as did the principal of my new school. I thanked them all for coming, and to our honored guests Henry and Larry, I said thank you for joining us.

"May I refer to you all by your first names?" All agreed

and said yes, I thanked them and started the workshop.

I said, "to start with, I would like all of you to step out in the hall and come in one at a time."

They did and I greeted each one separately as they came in calling them by their first names, and made each one feel special. I began by treating them as though they were my students. After I did this and we are now together,

I continued. "I am Mr. Frank, and I am your teacher for this class. Now, I am responsible to teach you Social Studies and how I do that is first of all, I don't give homework. You will learn all you need to know in this class, and I grade on the basis of how you show respect to your fellow students and myself."

"You will find that all of you will be rewarded for how you respond in this class also. I have given you name tags and I want you to write your names on them and wear them. The purpose for this is so I can get acquainted with you and also grade you on your performance. Oh yes, you will learn the subject but not in the traditional way. We are first going to learn respect for each other, and we are going to build relationships along with our lessons."

"You see it doesn't matter how much you learn or how smart you become, if you don't have respect, people will notice that right off and hire or not hire you on the basis of that."

As the class left I said to all of them, "Don't forget your name tags tomorrow, you will be graded on whether you have them or not."

"I am going to stop here for a moment and see if you have any questions. Yes, what is your question?"

"Well, I wanted to know how you came across this method?"

"That is a very good question, and I will tell you it was from my students in Henry's school. One day I was called to his office to talk to him and I had to leave the class, so I said to the class, "Just don't tear up the place while I am gone."

"When I came back the class had elected someone to continue teaching the subject, and that person took over and taught the class. So when I returned I didn't take it back, I saw an opportunity to show respect to the student who was teaching. I just went and sat in one of the desks and let the student finish out the time. Well, I graded the whole class that day, and they all got "A's". The children are still learning the subject and are very eager to learn, the parents are witnessing the change as well. They are even showing more respect at home. Now, all through my sharing with you I have only referred to the students as children not kids, they deserve more respect than we sometimes give them."

At the end I asked if there were any more question? "Yes, what is it Henry, what's your question?"

"I want to know if we can have another time, and this time have each teacher do this, and see if their personality will have the same results."

"Good question, how many want to do this" Everyone did so we set up another time.

I could see the value in doing this, as it would show that no matter what personality you had this would still work. But I would preface this by saying that we should always show that we care no matter what, and have a smile on our faces, too.

Chapter 16
Summer events

*I*t's summer break now and a time to get chores done that we started, for example our new house. It is almost finished, just the appliances need to be installed. Mia and I have decided on what we want, the floors have to be done yet, but we are almost there. In the meantime, we have the clients to help and more learning for me.

Sally is with us on the ranch almost every day now that school is out, and we love having her. She is so outgoing and fun to work with, and has been with us enough to know what to do with little direction. We gave her a horse to care for, so she is teaching him tricks now. He follows her around wherever she goes.

Sally's mom and dad come out on some weekends and go for rides with Sally. When we were out backpacking with my class, I told them we would have them come two at a time during the summer.

I will do that after we get back from our trip, to direct them, and Sally will be a big help with that too. This again could not be successful if the students didn't learn respect for each other, I don't see a problem with her doing some of the training. I am looking forward to this, we will invite a boy and a girl, and it will be teaching them to respect each other in the workplace.

Mom and Mia are making curtains and drapes for our new house, and I am laying the floors. I already put 12x12 marble on the walls in the shower and tubs.

The landscaper has come and is doing the work on the outside around the house. Now we are making plans to go to Maui for our first anniversary, and as I said before, we are taking Henry and Mom too. All the arrangements were made in advance so we leave on Monday. We are all ready to leave and be in town at the airport early. We are all excited, as the two of them have never been there before.

We arrived in Maui and are all up in our rooms, Mom and Henry have separate rooms overlooking the ocean. It is so beautiful and we all have dinners together, sometimes the two of them go off on their own. They would go, as we encouraged them to, on rides and took a helicopter ride to see all the area while Mia and I went surfing with surfboards. You remember we learned that from before when we were here on our honeymoon. Mia and I went on hikes that Mom and Henry were not up to. So we just had a great time and gave each other space to be on our own.

We all took a lot of pictures, and it will be a time to remember. We rented a car so we could go all over the island, and really get the most out of our time.

Henry surprised me, he had gotten a trip for the two of us to go fishing, and Mom had plans for Mia to have a mom and daughter time together. Henry and I got on the boat—they furnished all the fishing gear and the bait too.

So we went way out at sea and sat instead of trolling, it was said that we would do that on the way back. We got our lines out and were just sitting around, when all of a sudden both Henry and I got a fish on our poles. Oh wow, mine flew out of the water! It turned out to be a tuna fish and a legal size to keep. And Henry brought his in too, also legal size. We got our lines out there again and sat and sat, nothing. But that was all right with us, what we caught was enough to take home and feast on.

We got back and the skipper had a way of sending the fish home in dried ice with our flight home. We got back and told the ladies what we caught, and they were excited for us.

So what did you gals do? To which they replied, you'll see later what we did. That night before dinner the ladies dressed up in the clothes they bought, they were Hawaiian dresses. We danced and enjoyed the entertainment, but now it's time to get packed again. It was a great time together, but now it's time to go back home and remember the good times.

We are home and I set a schedule for my class to come over, two at a time. I will send their names in their e-mail to respond back. The two for tomorrow are all set to go and will be here for breakfast. Sally always comes for breakfast on Saturdays now, so I called her to let her know we are home.

She will be coming through the week now. She is learning about animal husbandry with Mia's help as she wants to be a veterinarian, and so she is getting hands-on training. Sally helped a while back with the birthing a calf and loved it. Mia is now training her on different phases of animal care.

We have been home now for a few weeks and have had the two student teams come and now we are starting over, but with different couples. In this way we are teaching togetherness, and it's working. Gertrude is taking the girls, after they do some chores with the horses, and teaching them to knit and sew. This is quite an experience. I take the boys and show them how to clean the horse's hooves, to get the dirt out that builds up from riding them in the dirt.

Well, on the night after dinner in our own house, Mia announced that she is pregnant. I was blown away, and got out of my chair, grabbed her up and was swinging her around I was so happy.

"Mia, Mia this is a very happy day in my life. How far along are you?"

Mia said two months, so I said I am thrilled, I wished I had a mother and father to share the news with.

Mia said, "I only have Mom so we will have to adopt some grandparents so our children will have some." I am so happy I won't be able to sleep tonight. "Let's go and tell Mom, will she ever be happy!"

It was Friday night and of course Henry was there too. So we took Mom aside and told her first, and she made such a racket that Henry came in to see what it was about. Mom asked if she could tell him.

Henry said, "did you win the lottery or something?"

Mom was dancing all around the place. Well, Henry

said, "Gertrude tell me what's going on!"

"My kids are going to have a baby that's what is going on." Henry said, "I was wondering when that would happen, now I will have a grand baby."

"Henry we were just talking about that, as I don't have any parents and Mia doesn't have a dad. She said that we are going have to adopt some."

Henry said, "I would be honored to be one."

When he said this, Gertrude looked at him as if to say, "What does that mean?" She didn't utter a word, but if looks could kill he would have been dead.

I said, "now we will have to redo the one bedroom for blue or pink, maybe I could paint with both colors then it wouldn't matter."

Mia said, "that is a great idea, and on one side we can put boy stuff and on the other side girl stuff. We don't even have to do an ultrasound to see what it is going to be, that way we can be surprised. Mia said, I don't like ultrasounds anyway, to put our baby in jeopardy that way. "Thanks Honey, I just love you," and Mom said, "me too."

We spent some time together throwing some names around for both boys and girls. It was getting late so Henry and Mom said goodnight and went to Mom's house.

I said to Mia, "Did you see how Mom looked at Henry when he said that he would like to be the grandpa? I would love to be a mouse in the corner when they get to the house; I wonder if there will be an announcement soon. I for one would love that, how about you Mia."

"I would love that too as I am no longer in the house like I was before we got married, it would help Mom not feel so lonely anymore." We both tried to include her in most things and I understand that's nice, but not like having someone next to you when you wake up.

It is Sunday now, and as usual we had breakfast together. Well, Henry said to Mom, "do you want me to tell them or do you want to?" Mia and I looked at each other with a smile on our face, and we were kind of snickering to ourselves as we suspected something already.

So they went aside and came back and they said it together, "we are ENGAGED."

"Well, we wondered how long it was going to take."

Both of us ran over and gave them both a hug and said congratulations.

Mom said, "See my ring!"

"Well, now with all the showers, we are all going to get wet for sure. Your mom and I talked it over, and we just want a simple wedding."

I said, "you know that's not going to happen. With this town and your school, too, Henry; when they hear this, oh man it will not be simple. Do you have a date in mind?"

"I thought August the 7th," Henry said. "We are so happy for you two, and it's a plus having you, Henry, to be my Dad now. Mom you made a good choice, and I know the relationship will grow. I now have a father and a mother, and a grandpa and grandma for our children."

"May I, as your son and friend, give you two some advice?" Both said. "hmm?" So I said, "don't think of this as a second marriage; don't forget your earlier spouses but don't compare the two of them either. You are on a new journey together to finish out the rest of your lives together. This is a second chance given to you, and as a couple, your lives are going to be enhanced for an example for others to see. I wouldn't be surprised if you will be sought after for advice now as a couple rather than singles. People don't know how to respond to singles, I know that by experience."

"Let others share in this new union and the memories will be so great to share with children and grandchildren too, I am excited to show you off"

Mia entered in by saying that I agree with your son, Mom. "I just love saying that," she said, "your son." Now, Mia went on, "I, too, have a dad I will remember. My dad is in heaven and he is looking down with his approval, he always wanted Mom to be happy. It's been a while now since I have seen Mom glow like she is right now. My heart is extremely happy, all the losses are being filled."

"Let's pray right now," I said, "to thank our heavenly Father for this upcoming union, and ask His blessing over it." We all prayed and thanked the Lord for putting us all together; I said, "Thank you Lord for giving me a family," and I broke down as I said that, and they were tears of joy.

We went to be at the gathering place this time in the car, and Henry and Mom talked to the preacher before the service; they told him they are engaged. After the message he said, "I think Henry and Gertrude have something they want to share with us."

They stood and went to the front of the group, and announced that they are getting married on August the 7th. Everyone applauded and they sat down, but the preacher said, "I don't think we are through making announcements are we?"

Mia and I stood in place and Mia said, "Frank and I are going to have a new addition besides having Henry join our family, we are going to have a baby." Now all the townspeople know what is going to happen in our family.

After the service men and women alike came to us and almost crushed us with hugs wanting to share in our happiness.

Then the unthinkable happened, the preacher said, "I am taking all of you out to lunch to celebrate these two couples' joyous events."

The women all got together and gave Mia a baby shower, while the men invited me to one of their houses where we got to know each other better. It was a great time and of course Henry was there, he will never be left out of anything again.

Several weeks later the whole town gave Gertrude a bridal shower, that is the ladies of the town. We guys went bowling and that was a great time together too.

Well, it's several months later and getting time for Mia to go and receive our bundle of joy.

One night she said, "it's time to go."

"Where?" I said.

"To the hospital, you goof." You know I painted the room with both colors, so what do you think happened? Yep! The doctor said when a son came there was another little person who wanted to come too, and it was a girl.

Mia had twins, one of each. So I guess I have to say, be careful what you paint the baby's room. Both are blonds and I have to say beautiful, but most of all healthy. Mom is doing great too, and you talk about glow, wow!

For Mia and I, life couldn't be better. It has definitely changed and we are going back to learning again, but life is full of that. We did arrive at different stations in life but we can't stay there, we must get on the train to experience more of life. I, for one, am ready.

Well, it's August and just days before a wedding. I asked Gertrude and Henry if I could marry them. They said we were talking about me doing that, but I'm not a preacher. I have already looked into it and all I have to do is go to the District Attorney and be deputized for the day.

"That is great, I can't think of anyone I would rather have perform it," Henry said, and Mom agreed.

Mom still had her wedding dress and just made a few changes to make it special. Mia helped and she is going to be the matron of honor, and Henry's son is going to be the best man. This is going to be a family event, how great is that?

Remember what Henry said, that he just wanted a simple wedding, well that never happened. The townspeople all got together and decorated the area around the lake we built. It is now gorgeous with trees, bushes and all kinds of flowers the girls planted, and ducks swimming around the lake.

We got six hundred chairs and placed them nicely to get the best effect for this occasion. Bruce came into the picture to help, you remember Ken's dad the dentist. What he did will set you on your ears. He organized the bands from both of our schools, Henry's and mine, to come and play before everything started. He found a famous female singer, and also a guy who played guitar and sang "Country Roads". (John Denver's song)

Bruce put this up on a large screen to make it the best it could be.

This was the most exciting time to pull town, country,

schools, community, and believers together to celebrate two people who contributed a lot to all our lives.

We had the buggy all decorated for their departure and Henry's horse to draw it.

Now it's time to perform the wedding; we are all ready for the bride to come down the aisle, and here she comes— so beautiful, led by our Vietnam veteran who has come a very long way.

The rest of us in the wedding party were all so emotional as we witnessed the scene of both coming down the aisle so happy; beautiful Gertrude in her gorgeous gown and Jake in his outfit. Jake is a quality person and now he knows it, it doesn't seem we can stop doing our job no matter what else we are doing.

They came up to where Henry and his son were, Jake gave Gertrude's hand to Henry, and then he (Jake) kissed her. I loved the sight and continued with my part.

I pronounced them husband and wife and said, "You may now kiss the bride." I then introduced them as Mr. and Mrs. Henry Smith. We all danced, Henry first, then me. Jake came over and took Gertrude from me, and every one moved off to allow them full freedom. We all applauded as they were doing so well and by now, everyone knew Jake and where he came from.

Now we are having dinner, catered by the local restaurants. We have witnessed a lot of help and volunteers who came to our rescue. This whole community is bonding together, what a privilege it is to be a part of this.

We are all saying good bye to the lovebirds as they go off in the horse and buggy.

They will take it to town and go from there by car to go on their honeymoon. I went and rescued the twins; they did great all through the ceremony. Mia was prepared to go and get them, but didn't have to. Our built-in baby sitter was Sally, of course. We might as well adopt her, she is so much a part of our family already.

Now we have the ranch all to ourselves, and of course all the chores, but we do have help. We haven't been alone ever since we got married. Tomorrow we go to meet with the church and that is going to be interesting as we will have the twins with us. Others have babies there too, so it is expected that we would do this. The preacher asked me if I would like to share the pulpit with him today and I accepted.

I had been interested in twins in the Bible, as to who were twins and how they grew together. So this is what I found:

1. Jacob and Esau

"These two brothers are certainly the best-known set of twins in Scripture. Isaac, the son of Abraham, and his wife, Rebecca, are the first couple mentioned in the Bible to have twins."

Genesis 25:22–26 says,

The babies jostled each other within her, and she said, 'Why is this happening to me?' So she went to inquire of the Lord. The Lord said to her, 'Two nations are in your womb, and two peoples from within you will be separated; one people will be stronger than the other, and the older will serve the younger." When the time came for her to give birth, there were twin boys in her womb.

The first to come out was red, and his whole body was like a hairy garment; so they named him Esau. After this, his brother came out, with his hand grasping Esau's heel; so he was named Jacob.

2. Cain and Abel: It is possible Cain and Abel were twins, but the Bible does not explicitly indicate this. It depends on how much later Abel was born: "Eve became pregnant and gave birth to Cain ... Later she gave birth to his brother Abel."

Genesis 4:1-2

3. Thomas Didymus: The Gospel of John notes that Thomas was called Didymus, a Greek word meaning, "twin"

John 11:16

The name Thomas also means "twin" in Aramaic, a common language of Jesus' time. This likely indicates that Thomas was one of two twin brothers.

John 20:24

"Twins are very special they will be watchful for each other throughout their lives, not as just young children, but also all through life. I was interested, as we have our twins, to see what to expect. But folks, I want to share with you that the Bible tells us that as children of God we will be heir and joint heirs with the Lord. So we, too, have a special place in God's family."

Chapter 17
Getting back to life

$\mathcal{M}$om and Dad are back from their honeymoon and we've all returned to our chores. I have two students here today so Sally took the girl, and I took the boy to mend fences. Now I am being sensitive to Mia's new job as she is used to being outdoors and now has to care for the twins.

When Mia has a client come she has Sally and me to help, so we switch off, we are all making an adjustment. We're enjoying the twins so much, I still have to laugh at the fact that I painted the baby's room with both colors. They blame me for having a boy and a girl, I guess that's true.

It sure was a good idea to build a new house though as it would be hard now with what happened, but Gertrude and Henry want to have a bed and breakfast business again. We are advertising the business and we are going to have people come, and so many more opportunities on the horizon.

The plaque that the Army gave us will be a drawing card for us. People will also be exposed to horse therapy and for those who want to ride, we will make that available too. Henry has fit right in and is thinking of quitting his job as a principal. I counseled him to think about staying in the educational area, as his experience is so valuable.

He said, "but it's an hour both ways to go into town."

"Let's pray about it" I said, "something will come up."

Well, as usual the Lord came aboard and the principal of the elementary school in our town wanted to move into the town where Henry was principal. Henry and the superintendent had a meeting and he suggested they do a switch, so now Henry is principal in our town. This is perfect, another answer to prayer. Now Henry and I can ride our horses together to school. If he switched with my principal, Henry would be my boss, which would be all right, I have a great amount of respect for him.

Henry's first day at work was a disaster, the children were uncontrollable.

Henry called me and said, "Frank, what can we do?"

I told him that I would come over between classes to observe and see if I could figure out a solution. The next day I rode my horse over to Henry's school and it was recess time. I got off Trigger and proceeded to show the children how to pet him, so they all got to pet Trigger. I told the children that if they were good and behaved themselves, I would let them come to the ranch and I would teach them how to ride, with their parents' permission.

"I will be listening to your teachers and if you are not behaving, I will not do it."

I went to the office to talk to Henry and tell him what I did.

"That's great Frank," he said. "I will let you know how that works, thanks, see you at home."

We're really busy having children from school come out to the ranch, but if we can stop them before they grow into being problems, I guess it's worth it.

Sally has been a great help and we have been blessed to have her with us. I like working with the young people in middle school because they are just entering into adolescence when there are a lot of changes happening in them. This is a very critical time for them to have a lot of good direction in their lives. I am glad that when I went through it I had a father to take me under his wing, so to speak. For example, it was then that I saw girls in a different light, and he taught me that they have value and to respect them.

They are not to be used and then just thrown away.

He was the closest thing I had to a father, so I listened to him and drank in all his instruction like a sponge. We as educators have the opportunity to see this and come alongside of them, girls as well as boys. This is where we can shine by involving ourselves in their lives. That is where coming out on the ranch really makes a difference. We have given them something else to divert their thinking. I have known children whose parents told them that they would never amount to anything, maybe because of being frustrated during this time of the changes in their children. The children for some reason will even buy into it and prove the parent right. We get them at this point and have the privilege in turning that around. So Frank, you might be saying as the reader, you are not hired to do that, you are supposed to be teaching reading, writing, and arithmetic and leave the other to the parents, right?

Wrong answer. Now I will ask you a question, how do we get them to learn when they have such low self-esteem? And when they buy into, "You will never amount to anything." These are quite often the cutups in class. This is where my method has been a success because through showing them respect, I am being like the man that took me in and taught me to respect myself first. I would have been the cutup in my class had he not done that. Now as a teacher I can get the subject that I was hired for into their minds. They now see they have value and the importance of learning to be all they can be. Through this method we have taken the rock off the hose.

Teachers sometimes come into children's lives where the parents leave off. I will try to bear this in mind now that I have my own. They will know that I not only love them, but respect them too. They say this is why grandparents are so important, it has been said that this is their second chance to do things right, where they messed up with their own children. So you might say that we as teachers are body and fender repairers, as we are helping to remove the dents and damage that our students experience from life. Why, after all, do children join gangs? They have found others who they have something in common with, maybe they are looking for love.

I have an investment in these fresh and moldable individuals, before they are gobbled up into these gangs, because they are looking for acceptance. That's why teaching self-respect works.

An interesting thing just happened, all three schools are together in developing quality individuals.

The three principals from elementary school, middle school, and now high school along with the superintendent and I, are together in meetings a lot. Elementary school because of Henry, of course middle school because that's where it all started. My students have graduated and are in high school, so now I am teaching high school teachers my methods—so it's continuing throughout our community.

I take no credit for the method; I give the credit to the Lord Jesus Christ. It's He that has developed this in me, because this is how the Lord treats me. I felt I was a throwaway kid, He showed me I had value and He loved me and died for me so I could live in heaven with Him. This is how the Lord showed to me that He respected me, and I am so happy to have Him in my life. Many of my students came to accept the Lord into their lives too, and He will carry them through life around all the evil things if they let Him do that for them.

Mia and I take our twins on rides and switch off holding them. They are growing and already showing individuality, this is going to be enjoyable to help direct them in life. The adult clients who are taking therapy are enjoying them too. The twins are learning to walk now and getting into things. The boy's name is John and the girl's name is Ruth, they love each other as they interact with one another. They just had their first birthday and love spending time with grandma and grandpa.

A new development has come about, remember I talked about the gangs in town? No, I am not bringing them to my ranch, at least not yet. But do you remember Jake the Vietnam Veteran? Well, he came for a visit and a ride, but really he wanted to talk to us about helping with the troubled kids in town. We talked it over, and I said I really have a full plate. Jake said he knew that, but thought he could do something, just needed some help to get started. I said I could do that by finding out if he can use the gym. Jake, of course, already knew the principal and was recognized as a valued person.

He was given permission to use the gym, so he went to where the gang met and said, "Who wants to play basketball?"

They all gathered around him to intimidate him. However, he was able to get them to listen to him by introducing himself and telling them how he lost his leg. He was appealing to their sensitive side, if they had one. Now they were all around him, to hear his stories, he was using his wheel chair to make an impact on them as he didn't need it anymore.

He went on to say that he put his life on the line, and was wounded, "So you young people could live in freedom to be whatever you want to be." He went on to say, "I hope I didn't waste my time and put my life on the line for nothing. So what about it, will you be on the court tomorrow? I will be there to teach you a good way of life, and have fun too."

The next day Jake was there and so was the gang, and they chose their teams. The school's team was prepared to oppose them, and Jake said, if there was any rough stuff it would be over. Now Jake is going to teach respect as he witnessed it on the ranch with Mia and how she worked with him and the horses. You say Jake is just wasting his time these kids are not going to change? Well, that's where you are wrong. I witnessed one of the gang helping one of the other team members up when he fell down. Jake is teaching them teamwork; no all stars, work together he told them.

All these guys wanted people to know they had value now. I know you are asking where the parents are, right? Some of them just had a drunk for a dad and were on their own.

Thanks to Jake they are not throwaway kids now. They are on their way to maybe someday, play on a major ball team. We were very thankful to see this change in our community. Townspeople are able to walk around and feel safe now, and the children from the gangs are even helping in the community, instead of being a nuisance.

The young people have discovered that they have value and they are not into drugs anymore, now we can reach them for the Lord too.

You, no doubt are saying, this sounds too good to be true, and you would be right. All that has taken place must be maintained carefully, it can't be all up to one person. It was great when Mia and I just had each other and were able to do some extra things, and now it's time for others to come along and put their shoulders to the efforts and the successful things that were being accomplished. It's like painting a house and maintaining it, or it will deteriorate. It will have a tendency to return to what it was before it was made so beautiful and preserved.

Years later:

There has been a lot going on, the twins are eight now and have their own horses. They're a great help around the ranch and are learning what Mom does in her business. They are also full of questions about how all of this happened in Mom's and Dad's life and how we got together. I tell them it was because of a flat tire. They look at both of us with a puzzled look on their face, Mia and I just smile at each other, and I reach over and give her a hug. The children see a lot of love in our family. This is so enjoyable, especially to me since I never had this growing up. I really appreciate this part of my life and I will never take it for granted, I will just accept what has been lavished on me.

I think of a time that we went on a ride in our Jeep up a trail. We came to a part of the road where we could not go back or forward, so we all had to get out and fill in the sides that had fallen off and left a void. We filled it with a lot of rocks so we could drive over it, and the kids all shouted as we drove over the spot we fixed. My life was like that, I couldn't go forward or back I was stuck. But in my case someone came along and filled that void so I could continue on with life and had direction, and He became my best friend. He is the Lord Jesus Christ.

No, this is not some religious book; it's our lives with our best friend in it is all. I wanted so much to share a life that was a mess and He took it and put it all together and you are just witnessing it with us. It has been a great life, even with its twist and turns. But we are never alone, our best friend is always with us in whatever is going on. Remember trust plus respect equals relationship? That's what this is. Can you imagine a relationship with the one who created everything including us?

What a blessing to have had twins who now look after each other, they are so special and will be in each other's lives forever.

Something unforeseen just happened, our friend Jake was rushed to the hospital. We sped over and were told he didn't make it. He had us as his family, no one else that we know of. It was a very sad day in our lives, the twins too, they wanted to know why God took him! We sat them down and explained that his job was over you know, he survived the war and struggled through much pain because of it. His heart could no longer endure the pain and gave up. But before he left, us you have to know He asked Jesus Christ into his heart so now he is in heaven where there is no more pain.

"Mom, Dad," John said, "I want to go there too and be with Jake again someday, can I just ask the Lord to come into me now?" "Yes, son," and then Ruth said, "I also want to." "You are twins, so just both of you at the same time pray: "Lord, I thank you for dying for me on the cross, please come into my heart." Both of them did that at the same time, so precious. We all cried for joy and had a family hug, I will remember that forever. Thank you, Jake, for your love to us.

I held the memorial, the governor opened in prayer, and each of the principals spoke and shared precious moments they remembered. The Army was there, and the band played in both the football field and at the cemetery. They also fired off ten rounds in appreciation of his service.

Do you know who else was there? Yep, the children he got off the street. The children with their families from high school, along with many of the townspeople, and his friends who had taken therapy with him. There were some in his regiment who also survived the war. We used the football field, as there were too many for a building. I was so overtaken that I was asked to do this for Jake. I was able to share the gospel, and let people know if they wanted to see Jake again that they would have to ask Jesus Christ into their heart. We opened up the mic for anyone to share and the first ones were our twins. They told how much they will miss him, he was a very large part of our lives.

John and Ruth both said at the same time, "We asked Jesus into my heart the day Jake died, we will see him again." When all was finished, I said that Jake is going to have a lot of rewards.

The gang Jake got off the street came up next and said, "We all want to be with Jake too, so we have talked it over and want to ask the Lord into our hearts."

There was not a dry eye in the place. I invited anyone who wanted to come up front and join with them to do that together now. A lot of folks came and were invited to just ask the Lord to come into their hearts. We gave them time to do that and then I asked Henry to close the event in prayer.

We had brought the wagon for the casket and the twins drove it. Mia and I rode our horses next to each other and Henry and Gertrude did the same, the mayors of our two cities next, and the principals behind them. The governor was in front of the wagon and the Army at the front of the procession with the veterans marching with them. It was a sight to see, and Jake earned every bit of it for what he did for our community.

What is truly incredible is that the governor made a bronzed statue of a wounded soldier holding a Bible and a flag, to be put up in the main part of town where Jake found the gang, to forever be a memory of the day Jake touched all our lives.

On the plaque it read. "To Jake, a man that loved God and his country." Jake served his God, his country and also his community, to leave us an example that changed how we think about people in need. May he enjoy his new home in Glory with his Lord and fellow soldiers that gave their lives for us!

Sometime later the pastor died, and as a group of believers we got together and said, "It's time that we step up and use our spiritual gifts, and not look to replace the man who taught us to be about our Father's business. Now we have a chance to do that, so we will look for those gifts among us.

"We were happy to hear that and responded to it. I began teaching, as did others like Bruce, Henry, and some of the other men in the congregation. The group said, now we can do things the right way as the scripture teaches us.

Even some of the young men from the gang are in the group and taking leadership roles to make this a very happy ending. The twins are home and working with us, Ruth is certified to work with Mia and John is adding other things to the ranch. He is increasing the herd of cattle and this is going to be his income.

Looks like we will be building more houses for Ruth and John eventually. Henry is backing off some and is now retired, so Gertrude and Henry are traveling some, and Mia and I are working with the bed& breakfast business.

I still think of the day on that dirt road and the young lady with a flat tire and just look at what happened with that. We love happy endings so I will leave it there. Thank you for allowing us in sharing our live with you; hope you have found yourselves in some part of the sequence as they happened. So the moral of the story is, it doesn't matter how you start in life, it important how you finish. Hope to see you all in Glory.

From all your loving friend's, Mia, Frank, Gertrude, Henry, Ruth, John, and Sally of course. And to all the others who contributed to making this a happy ending. May all your dreams come true, thanks for stopping by.

About the Author

*H*arold Thompson was born in Alameda, California. He moved to Reno, Nevada when his wife was going through cancer treatment. Since having lost a wife and three children to cancer, he has one son living in a neighboring state, whom he loves dearly.

Harold was an acting pastor for sixty-five years and a volunteer chaplain at San Quentin for five years.

While in the Army, he started a Christian group in Seoul, Korea. Harold was a contractor for many years and supported his family through this endeavor.

He has previously published two books, In All Thy Ways, Volume I and Volume II. When Dreams Come True came to Harold in a dream. It was a life changing experience.

In Harold's own word, "Of all the things I have done, this may be my finest hour. I am eighty-six years old, but still active. I have looked at my losses as my family's gain; they have gone before me to heaven, and they will be there to welcome me when it's my turn to go there."

Additional books available by Harold Thompson

"In All Thy Ways…"
>Volume I
>>Harold & Margaret Thompson

"In All Thy Ways…"
>Going It Alone, Volume II
>>Harold Thompson

Available at: LeRue Press
280 Greg Street #10
Reno, NV 89502
Lrpnv.com

Amazon.com

Barnes & Noble

Independent Bookstores

Kindle